12/20/13

Diamond Lake

19-1100

J 14113 L77

THOR

the challenge!

Writer: STAN LEE
Penciler: JACK KIRBY

Inker: VINCE COLLETTA
Colorist: MATT MILLA
Letterer: ART SIMEK

Cover Artists: OLIVIER COIPEL, MARK MORALES
& LAURA MARTIN

Collection Editors: MARK D. BEAZLEY & CORY LEVINE
Assistant Editors: ALEX STARBUCK & NELSON RIBEIRO
Editor, Special Projects: JENNIFER GRÜNWALD
Senior Editor, Special Projects: JEFF YOUNGQUIST
SVP of Print & Digital Publishing Sales: DAVID GABRIEL
Research: JEPH YORK & DANA PERKINS
Select Art Reconstruction: TOM ZIUKO
Production: JERRON QUALITY COLOR & JOE FRONTIRRE
Book Designer: SPRING HOTELING

Editor In Chief: AXEL ALONSO
Chief Creative Officer: JOE QUESADA
Publisher: DAN BUCKLEY
Executive Producer: ALAN FINE

SPECIAL THANKS TO RALPH MACCHIO

MARVEL

Spotlight

Visit us at www.abdopublishing.com

Reinforced library bound editions published in 2014 by Spotlight, a division of the ABDO Group, PO Box 398166, Minneapolis, MN 55439. Spotlight produces high-quality reinforced library bound editions for schools and libraries. Published by agreement with Marvel Characters, Inc.

Printed in the United States of America, North Mankato, Minnesota.
042013
092013
♻ This book contains at least 10% recycled material.

marvel.com

Library of Congress Cataloging-in-Publication Data

Lee, Stan.
  The challenge! / story by Stan Lee ; art by Jack Kirby.
     pages cm. -- (Thor, tales of Asgard)
  "Marvel."
  Summary: An adaptation, in graphic novel form, of comic books revealing the adventures of the Norse Gods and Thor before he came to Earth, featuring the relationship between young Thor and his scheming half-brother, Loki.
  ISBN 978-1-61479-171-3 (alk. paper)
1. Thor (Norse deity)--Juvenile fiction. 2. Graphic novels. [1. Graphic novels. 2. Thor (Norse deity)--Fiction. 3. Mythology, Norse--Fiction.] I. Kirby, Jack, illustrator. II. Title.
  PZ7.S81712Ch 2013
  741.5'973--dc23
                              2013005405

All Spotlight books are reinforced library bindings
and manufactured in the United States of America.

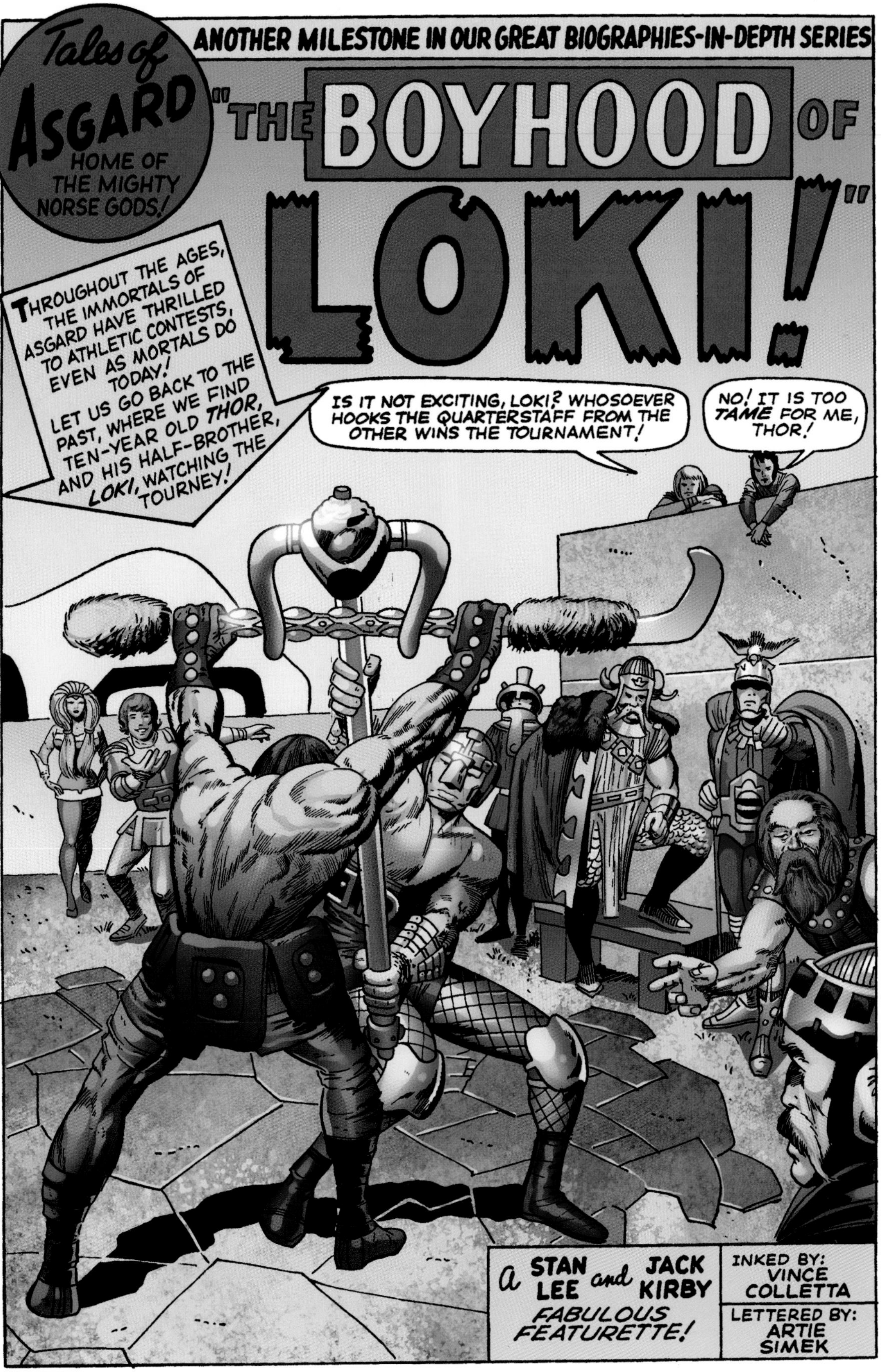
Tales of ASGARD HOME OF THE MIGHTY NORSE GODS!
ANOTHER MILESTONE IN OUR GREAT BIOGRAPHIES-IN-DEPTH SERIES
"THE BOYHOOD OF LOKI!"
THROUGHOUT THE AGES, THE IMMORTALS OF ASGARD HAVE THRILLED TO ATHLETIC CONTESTS, EVEN AS MORTALS DO TODAY! LET US GO BACK TO THE PAST, WHERE WE FIND TEN-YEAR OLD THOR, AND HIS HALF-BROTHER, LOKI, WATCHING THE TOURNEY!
IS IT NOT EXCITING, LOKI? WHOSOEVER HOOKS THE QUARTERSTAFF FROM THE OTHER WINS THE TOURNAMENT!
NO! IT IS TOO TAME FOR ME, THOR!
A STAN LEE and JACK KIRBY FABULOUS FEATURETTE!
INKED BY: VINCE COLLETTA
LETTERED BY: ARTIE SIMEK

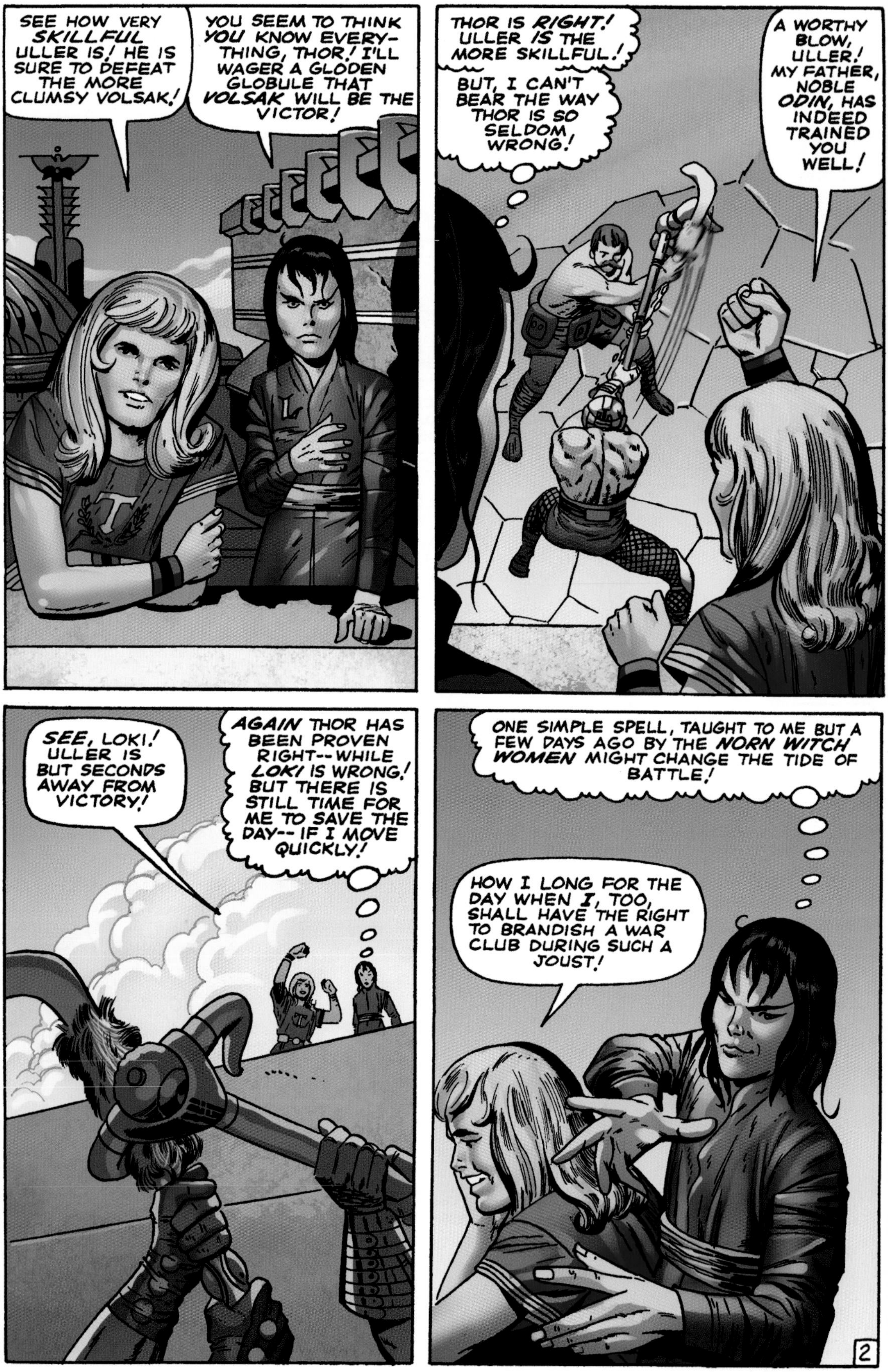
SEE HOW VERY SKILLFUL ULLER IS! HE IS SURE TO DEFEAT THE MORE CLUMSY VOLSAK!
YOU SEEM TO THINK YOU KNOW EVERY-THING, THOR! I'LL WAGER A GLODEN GLOBULE THAT VOLSAK WILL BE THE VICTOR!
THOR IS RIGHT! ULLER IS THE MORE SKILLFUL!
BUT, I CAN'T BEAR THE WAY THOR IS SO SELDOM WRONG!
A WORTHY BLOW, ULLER! MY FATHER, NOBLE ODIN, HAS INDEED TRAINED YOU WELL!
SEE, LOKI! ULLER IS BUT SECONDS AWAY FROM VICTORY!
AGAIN THOR HAS BEEN PROVEN RIGHT--WHILE LOKI IS WRONG! BUT THERE IS STILL TIME FOR ME TO SAVE THE DAY-- IF I MOVE QUICKLY!
ONE SIMPLE SPELL, TAUGHT TO ME BUT A FEW DAYS AGO BY THE NORN WITCH WOMEN MIGHT CHANGE THE TIDE OF BATTLE!
HOW I LONG FOR THE DAY WHEN I, TOO, SHALL HAVE THE RIGHT TO BRANDISH A WAR CLUB DURING SUCH A JOUST!
2

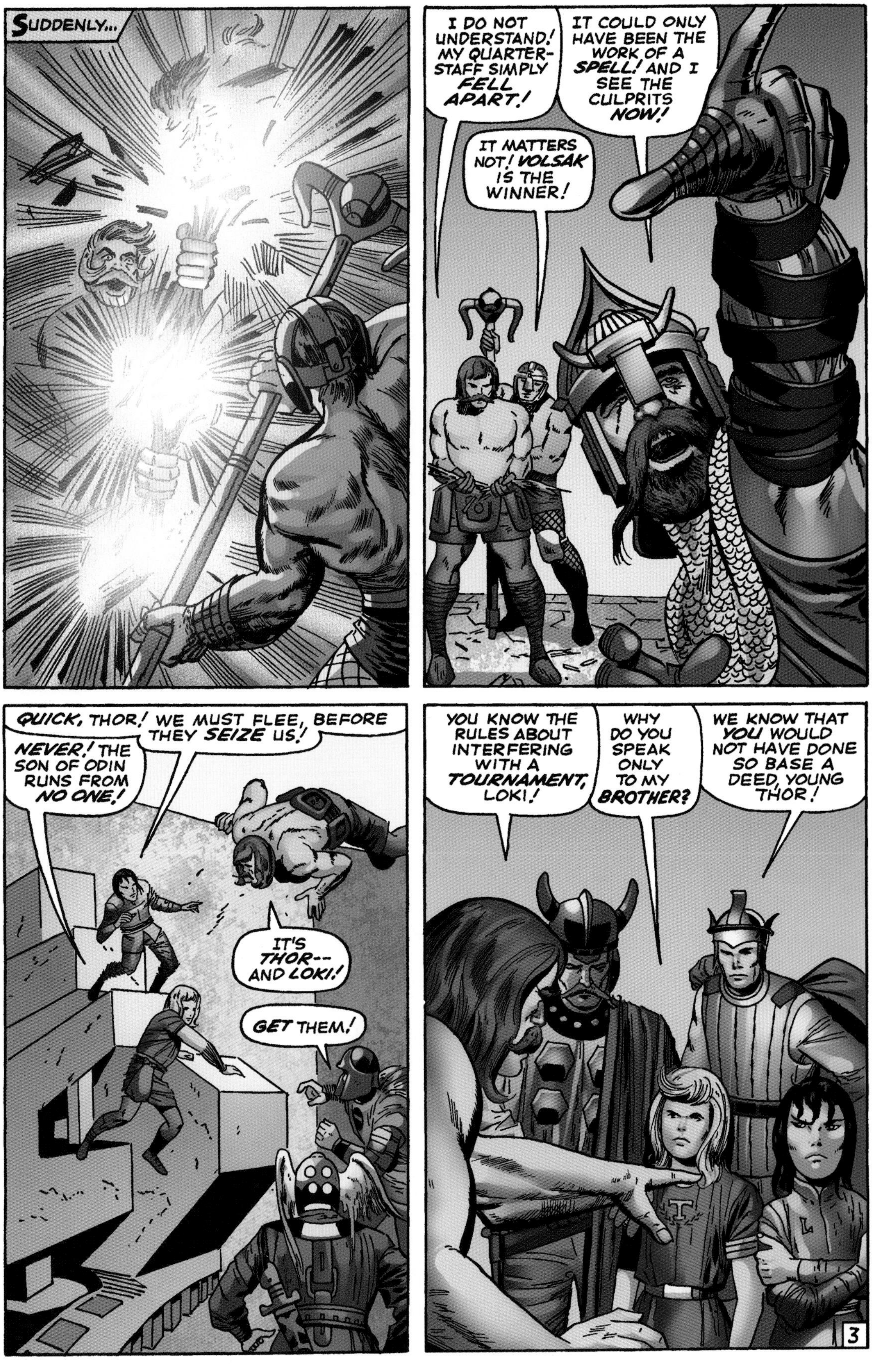
SUDDENLY...
I DO NOT UNDERSTAND! MY QUARTER-STAFF SIMPLY FELL APART!
IT MATTERS NOT! VOLSAK IS THE WINNER!
IT COULD ONLY HAVE BEEN THE WORK OF A SPELL! AND I SEE THE CULPRITS NOW!
QUICK, THOR! WE MUST FLEE, BEFORE THEY SEIZE US!
NEVER! THE SON OF ODIN RUNS FROM NO ONE!
IT'S THOR-- AND LOKI!
GET THEM!
YOU KNOW THE RULES ABOUT INTERFERING WITH A TOURNAMENT, LOKI!
WHY DO YOU SPEAK ONLY TO MY BROTHER?
WE KNOW THAT YOU WOULD NOT HAVE DONE SO BASE A DEED, YOUNG THOR!
3

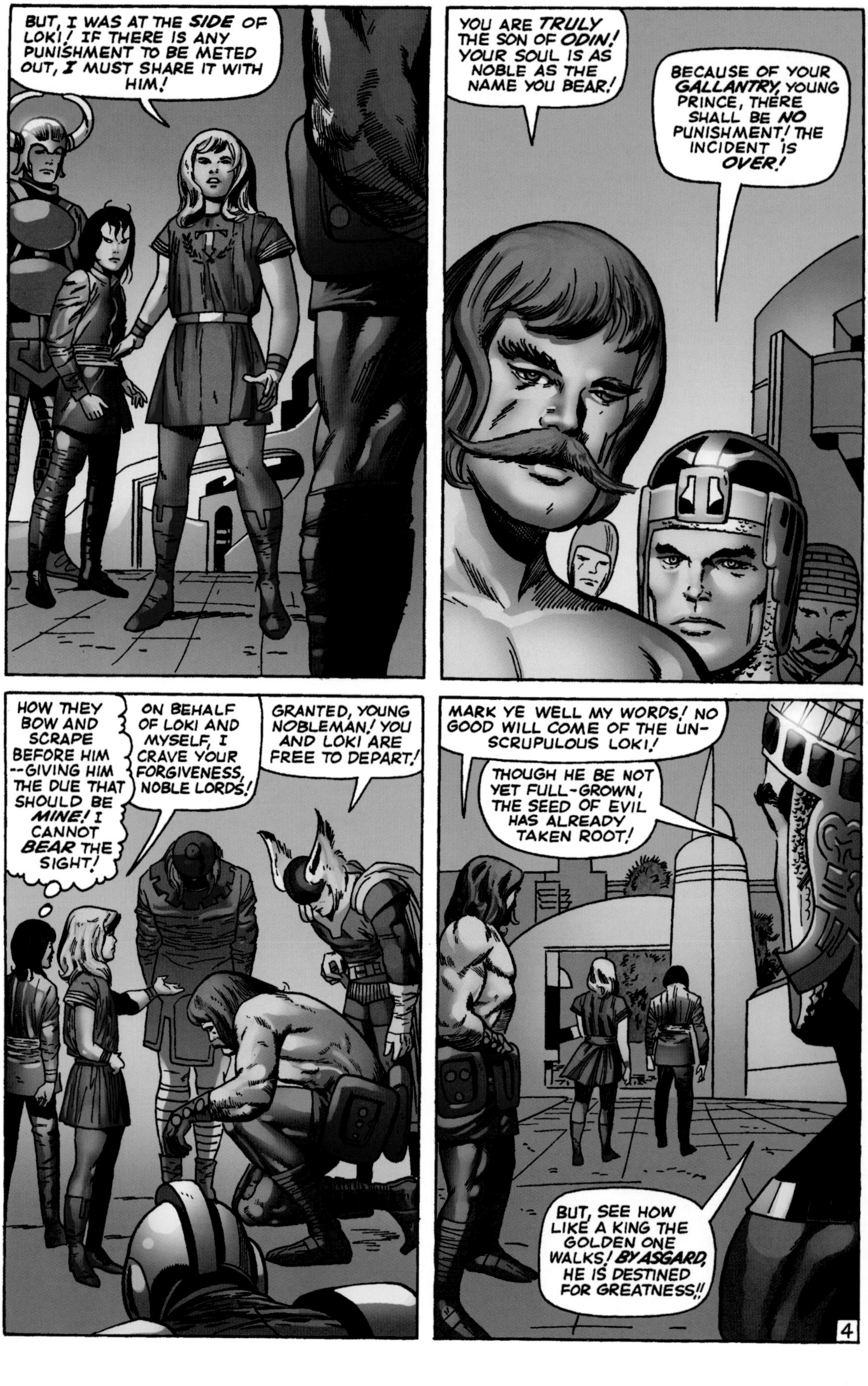
BUT, I WAS AT THE SIDE OF LOKI! IF THERE IS ANY PUNISHMENT TO BE METED OUT, I MUST SHARE IT WITH HIM!
YOU ARE TRULY THE SON OF ODIN! YOUR SOUL IS AS NOBLE AS THE NAME YOU BEAR!
BECAUSE OF YOUR GALLANTRY, YOUNG PRINCE, THERE SHALL BE NO PUNISHMENT! THE INCIDENT IS OVER!
HOW THEY BOW AND SCRAPE BEFORE HIM --GIVING HIM THE DUE THAT SHOULD BE MINE! I CANNOT BEAR THE SIGHT!
ON BEHALF OF LOKI AND MYSELF, I CRAVE YOUR FORGIVENESS, NOBLE LORDS!
GRANTED, YOUNG NOBLEMAN! YOU AND LOKI ARE FREE TO DEPART!
MARK YE WELL MY WORDS! NO GOOD WILL COME OF THE UN-SCRUPULOUS LOKI!
THOUGH HE BE NOT YET FULL-GROWN, THE SEED OF EVIL HAS ALREADY TAKEN ROOT!
BUT, SEE HOW LIKE A KING THE GOLDEN ONE WALKS! BY ASGARD, HE IS DESTINED FOR GREATNESS!!
4

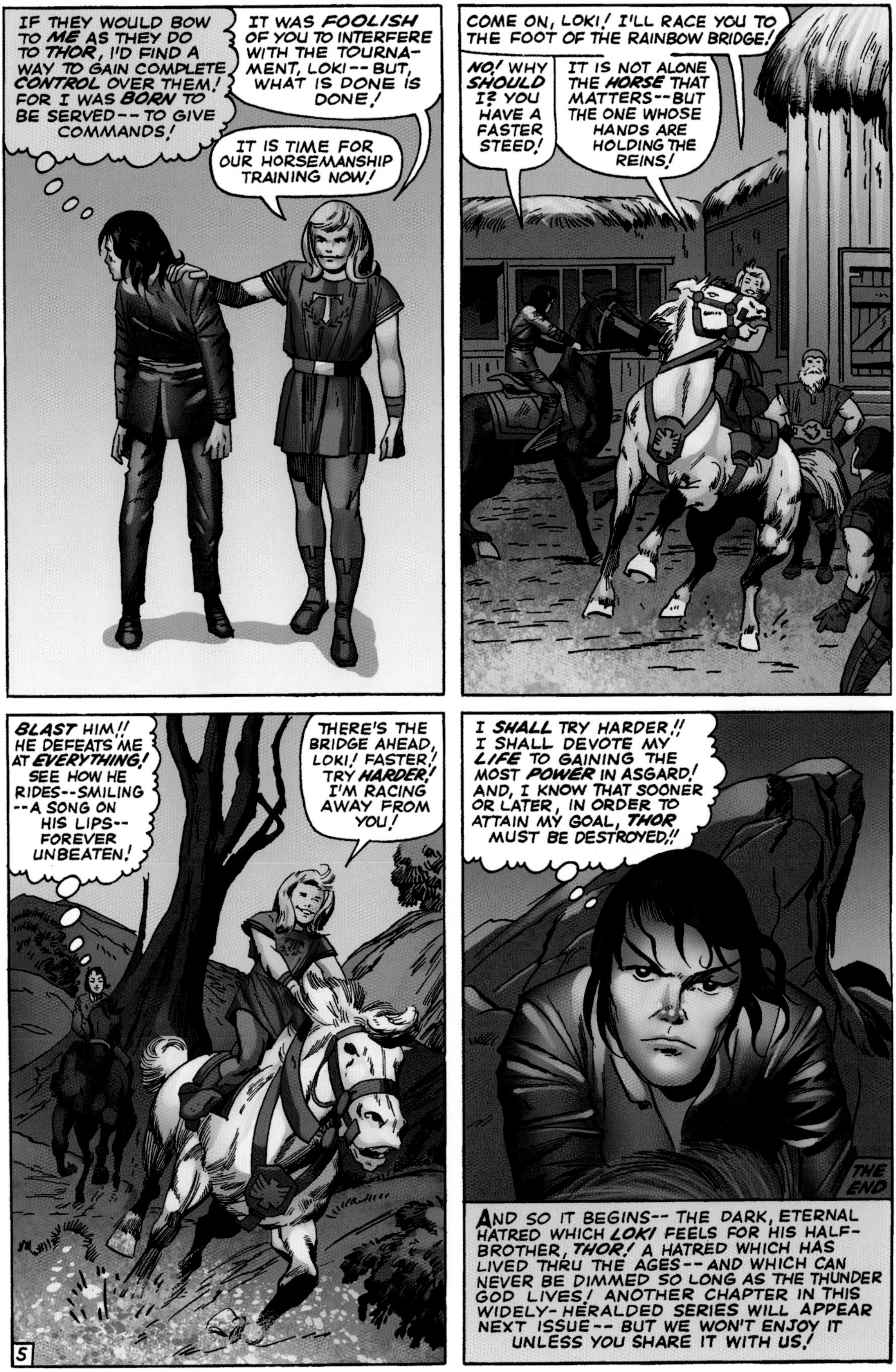

IF THEY WOULD BOW TO ME AS THEY DO TO THOR, I'D FIND A WAY TO GAIN COMPLETE CONTROL OVER THEM! FOR I WAS BORN TO BE SERVED -- TO GIVE COMMANDS!
IT WAS FOOLISH OF YOU TO INTERFERE WITH THE TOURNAMENT, LOKI -- BUT, WHAT IS DONE IS DONE!
IT IS TIME FOR OUR HORSEMANSHIP TRAINING NOW!
COME ON, LOKI! I'LL RACE YOU TO THE FOOT OF THE RAINBOW BRIDGE!
NO! WHY SHOULD I? YOU HAVE A FASTER STEED!
IT IS NOT ALONE THE HORSE THAT MATTERS -- BUT THE ONE WHOSE HANDS ARE HOLDING THE REINS!
BLAST HIM!! HE DEFEATS ME AT EVERYTHING! SEE HOW HE RIDES -- SMILING -- A SONG ON HIS LIPS -- FOREVER UNBEATEN!
THERE'S THE BRIDGE AHEAD, LOKI! FASTER! TRY HARDER! I'M RACING AWAY FROM YOU!
5
I SHALL TRY HARDER!! I SHALL DEVOTE MY LIFE TO GAINING THE MOST POWER IN ASGARD! AND, I KNOW THAT SOONER OR LATER, IN ORDER TO ATTAIN MY GOAL, THOR MUST BE DESTROYED!!
THE END
AND SO IT BEGINS -- THE DARK, ETERNAL HATRED WHICH LOKI FEELS FOR HIS HALF-BROTHER, THOR! A HATRED WHICH HAS LIVED THRU THE AGES -- AND WHICH CAN NEVER BE DIMMED SO LONG AS THE THUNDER GOD LIVES! ANOTHER CHAPTER IN THIS WIDELY-HERALDED SERIES WILL APPEAR NEXT ISSUE -- BUT WE WON'T ENJOY IT UNLESS YOU SHARE IT WITH US!

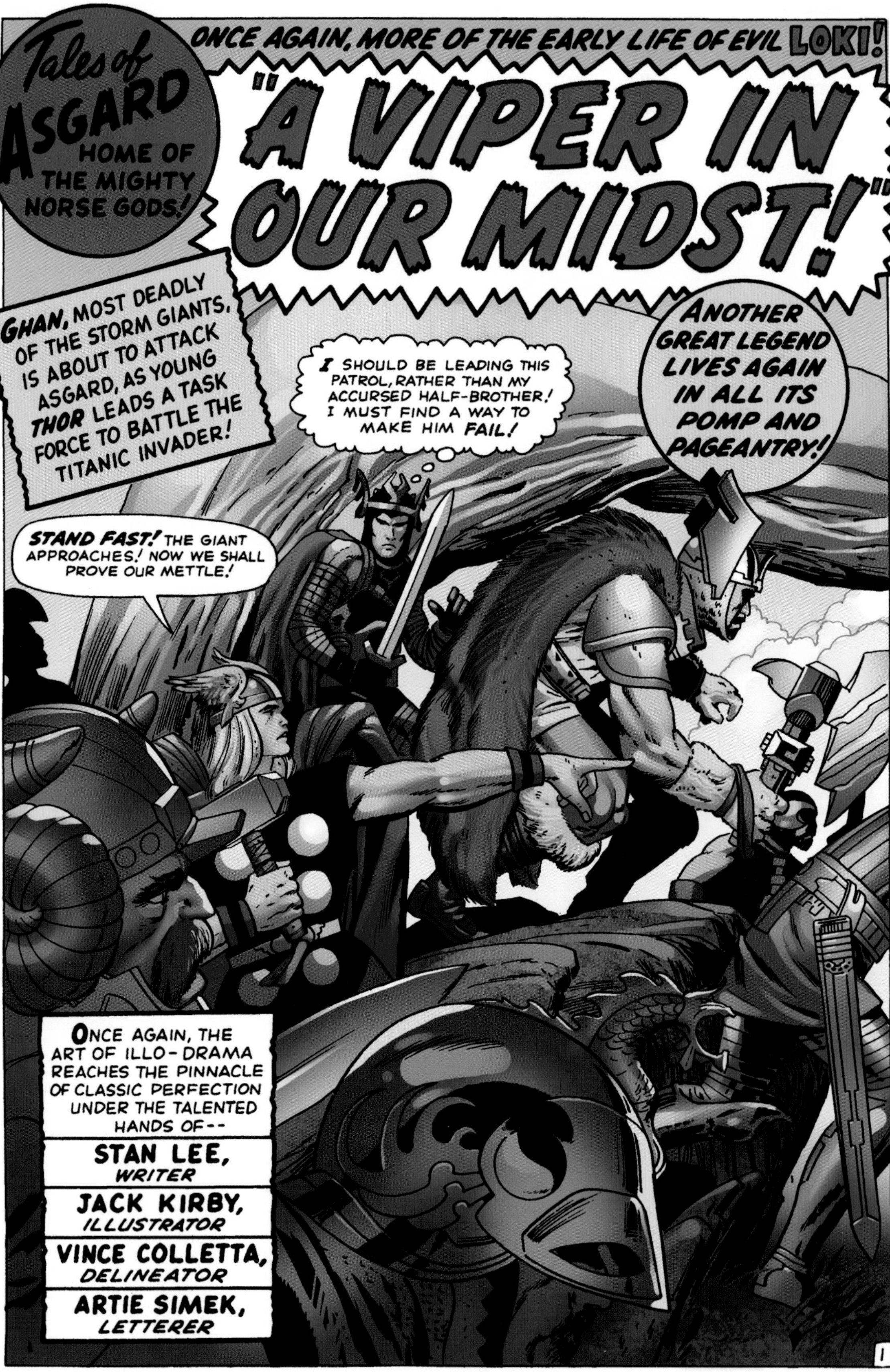
Tales of ASGARD HOME OF THE MIGHTY NORSE GODS!
ONCE AGAIN, MORE OF THE EARLY LIFE OF EVIL LOKI!
"A VIPER IN OUR MIDST!"
GHAN, MOST DEADLY OF THE STORM GIANTS, IS ABOUT TO ATTACK ASGARD, AS YOUNG THOR LEADS A TASK FORCE TO BATTLE THE TITANIC INVADER!
I SHOULD BE LEADING THIS PATROL, RATHER THAN MY ACCURSED HALF-BROTHER! I MUST FIND A WAY TO MAKE HIM FAIL!
ANOTHER GREAT LEGEND LIVES AGAIN IN ALL ITS POMP AND PAGEANTRY!
STAND FAST! THE GIANT APPROACHES! NOW WE SHALL PROVE OUR METTLE!
ONCE AGAIN, THE ART OF ILLO-DRAMA REACHES THE PINNACLE OF CLASSIC PERFECTION UNDER THE TALENTED HANDS OF--
STAN LEE, WRITER
JACK KIRBY, ILLUSTRATOR
VINCE COLLETTA, DELINEATOR
ARTIE SIMEK, LETTERER
1

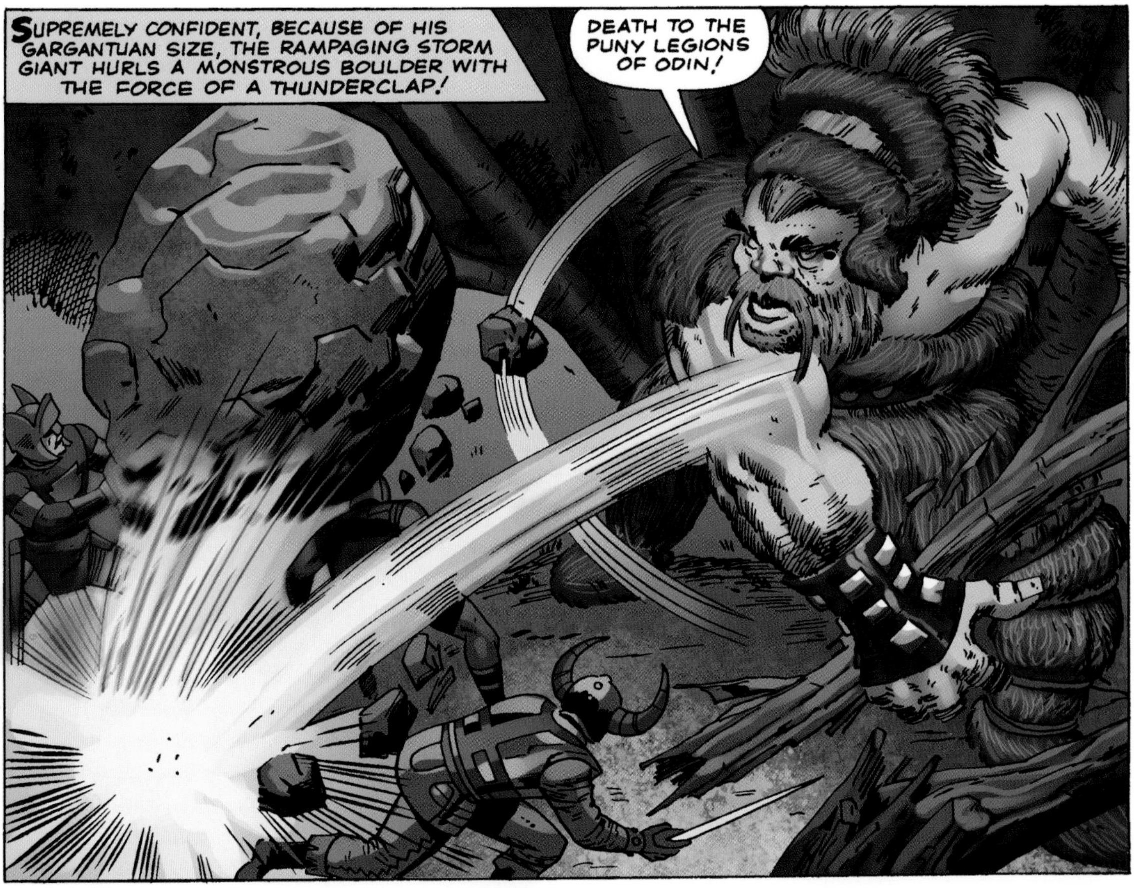
SUPREMELY CONFIDENT, BECAUSE OF HIS GARGANTUAN SIZE, THE RAMPAGING STORM GIANT HURLS A MONSTROUS BOULDER WITH THE FORCE OF A THUNDERCLAP!
DEATH TO THE PUNY LEGIONS OF ODIN!

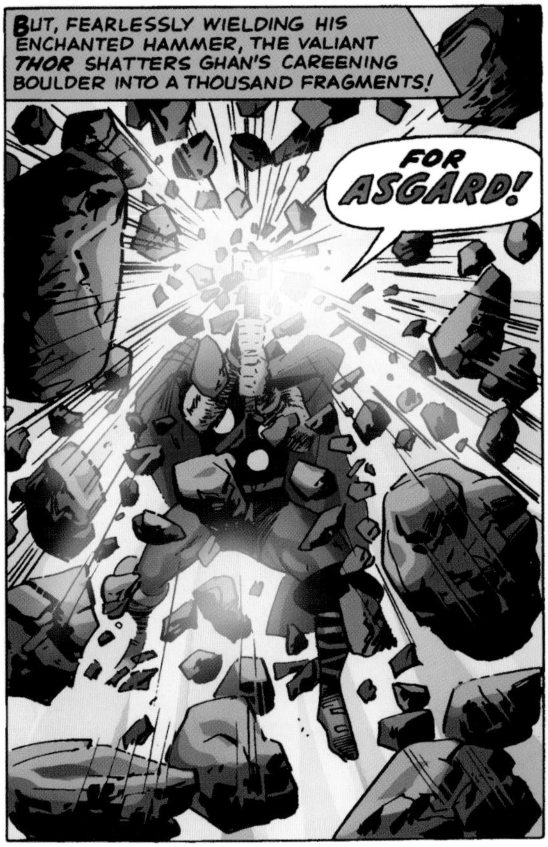
BUT, FEARLESSLY WIELDING HIS ENCHANTED HAMMER, THE VALIANT THOR SHATTERS GHAN'S CAREENING BOULDER INTO A THOUSAND FRAGMENTS!
FOR ASGARD!

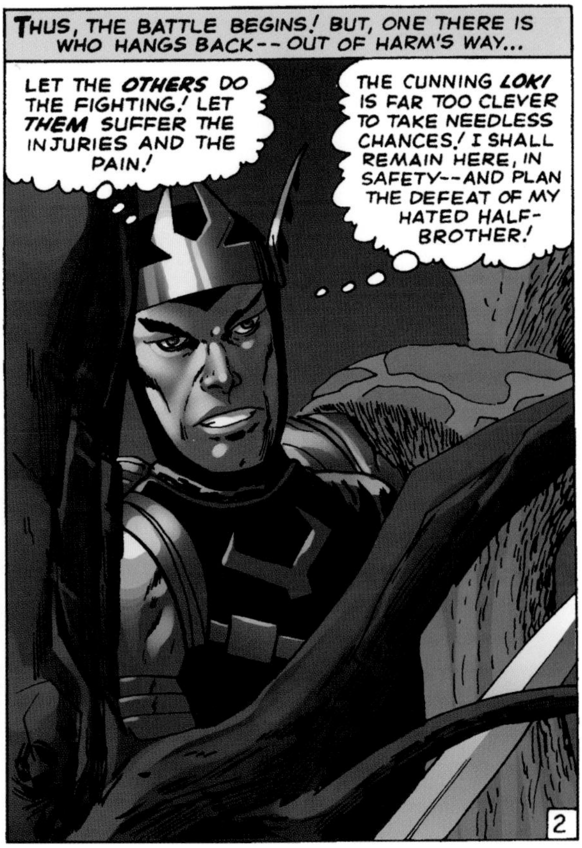
THUS, THE BATTLE BEGINS! BUT, ONE THERE IS WHO HANGS BACK-- OUT OF HARM'S WAY...
LET THE OTHERS DO THE FIGHTING! LET THEM SUFFER THE INJURIES AND THE PAIN!
THE CUNNING LOKI IS FAR TOO CLEVER TO TAKE NEEDLESS CHANCES! I SHALL REMAIN HERE, IN SAFETY--AND PLAN THE DEFEAT OF MY HATED HALF-BROTHER!
2

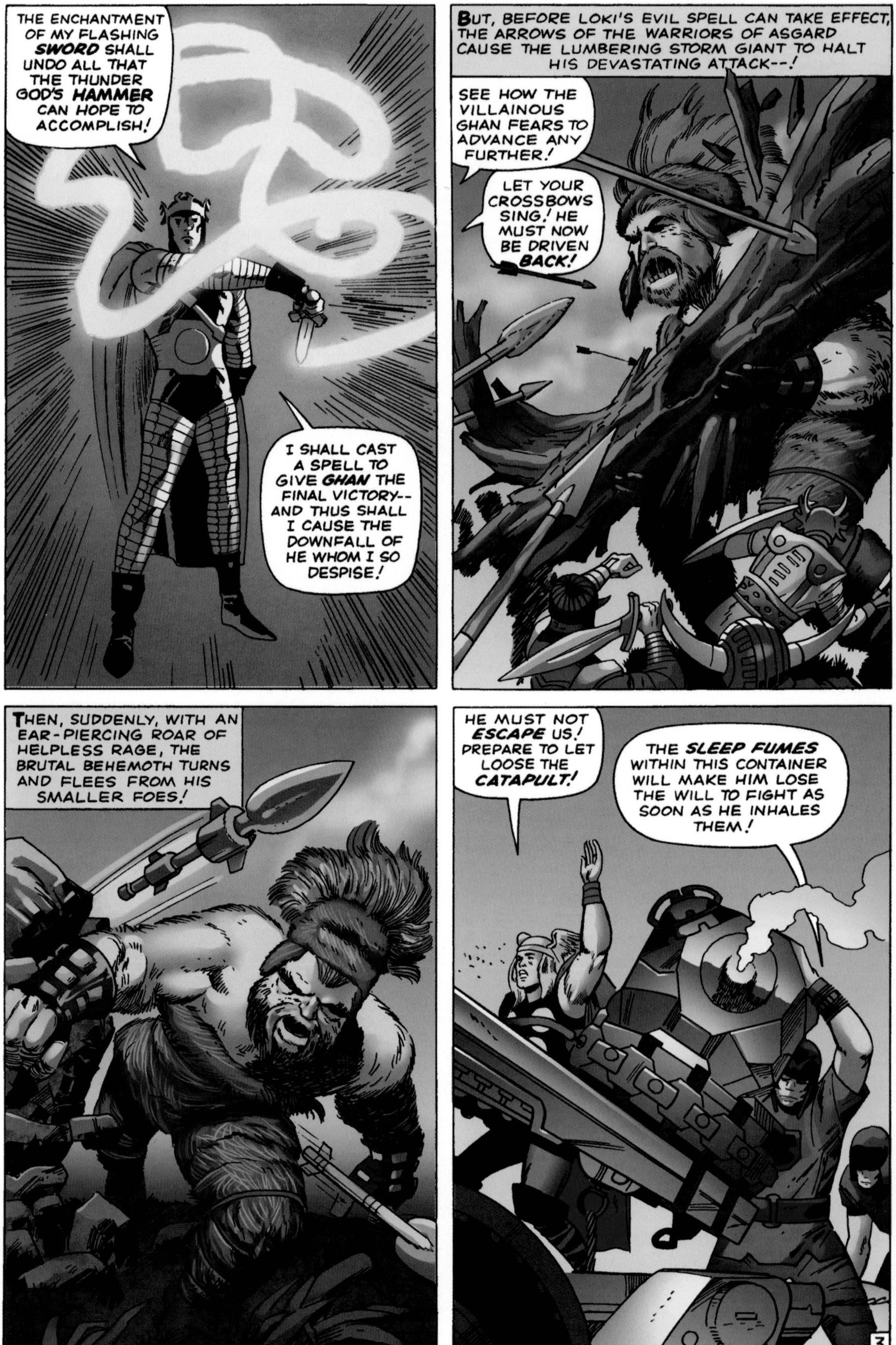
THE ENCHANTMENT OF MY FLASHING SWORD SHALL UNDO ALL THAT THE THUNDER GOD'S HAMMER CAN HOPE TO ACCOMPLISH!
I SHALL CAST A SPELL TO GIVE GHAN THE FINAL VICTORY-- AND THUS SHALL I CAUSE THE DOWNFALL OF HE WHOM I SO DESPISE!
BUT, BEFORE LOKI'S EVIL SPELL CAN TAKE EFFECT, THE ARROWS OF THE WARRIORS OF ASGARD CAUSE THE LUMBERING STORM GIANT TO HALT HIS DEVASTATING ATTACK--!
SEE HOW THE VILLAINOUS GHAN FEARS TO ADVANCE ANY FURTHER!
LET YOUR CROSSBOWS SING! HE MUST NOW BE DRIVEN BACK!
THEN, SUDDENLY, WITH AN EAR-PIERCING ROAR OF HELPLESS RAGE, THE BRUTAL BEHEMOTH TURNS AND FLEES FROM HIS SMALLER FOES!
HE MUST NOT ESCAPE US! PREPARE TO LET LOOSE THE CATAPULT!
THE SLEEP FUMES WITHIN THIS CONTAINER WILL MAKE HIM LOSE THE WILL TO FIGHT AS SOON AS HE INHALES THEM!
3

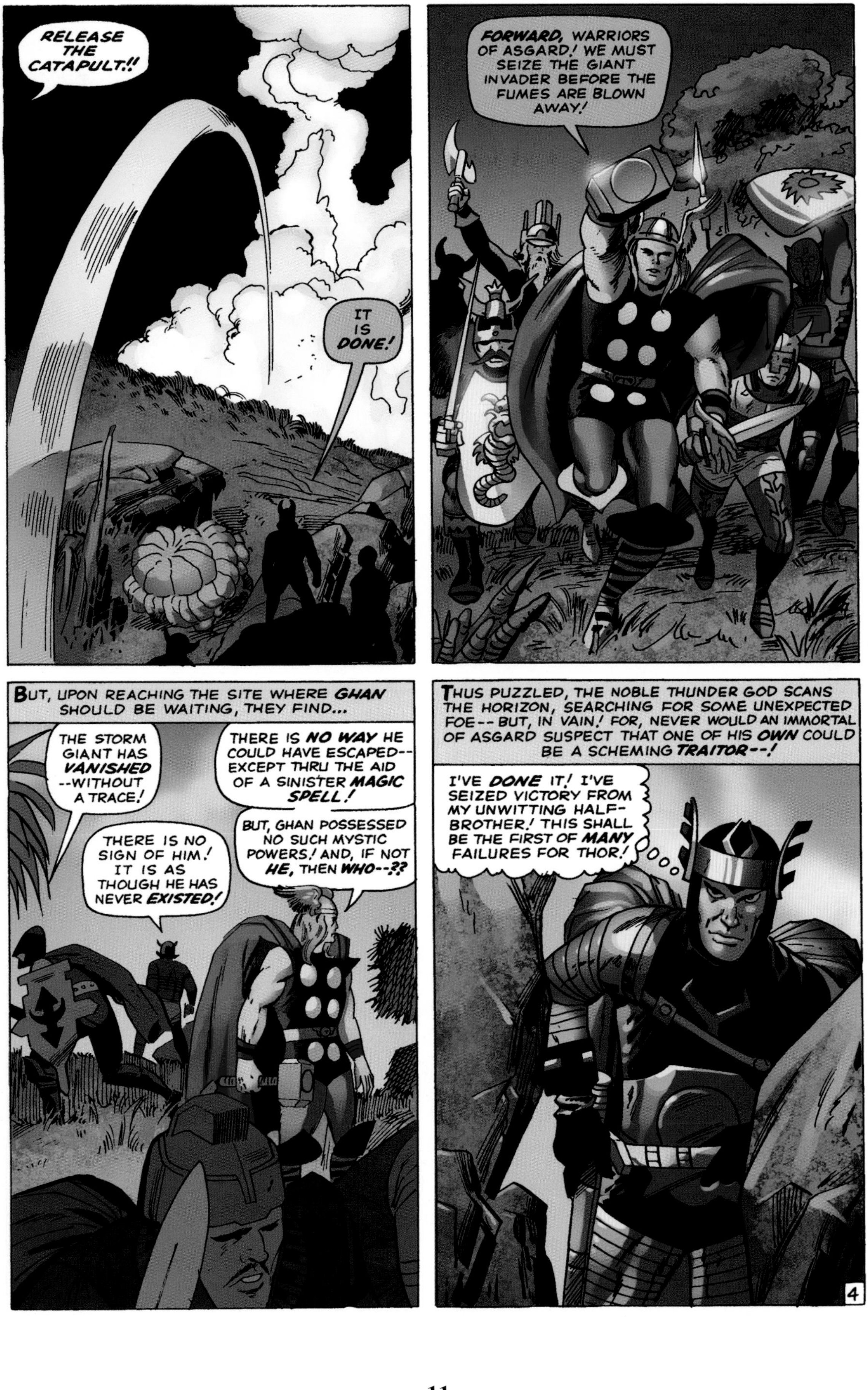
RELEASE THE CATAPULT!!
IT IS DONE!
FORWARD, WARRIORS OF ASGARD! WE MUST SEIZE THE GIANT INVADER BEFORE THE FUMES ARE BLOWN AWAY!
BUT, UPON REACHING THE SITE WHERE GHAN SHOULD BE WAITING, THEY FIND...
THE STORM GIANT HAS VANISHED --WITHOUT A TRACE!
THERE IS NO SIGN OF HIM! IT IS AS THOUGH HE HAS NEVER EXISTED!
THERE IS NO WAY HE COULD HAVE ESCAPED-- EXCEPT THRU THE AID OF A SINISTER MAGIC SPELL!
BUT, GHAN POSSESSED NO SUCH MYSTIC POWERS! AND, IF NOT HE, THEN WHO--??
THUS PUZZLED, THE NOBLE THUNDER GOD SCANS THE HORIZON, SEARCHING FOR SOME UNEXPECTED FOE-- BUT, IN VAIN! FOR, NEVER WOULD AN IMMORTAL OF ASGARD SUSPECT THAT ONE OF HIS OWN COULD BE A SCHEMING TRAITOR--!
I'VE DONE IT! I'VE SEIZED VICTORY FROM MY UNWITTING HALF-BROTHER! THIS SHALL BE THE FIRST OF MANY FAILURES FOR THOR!
4

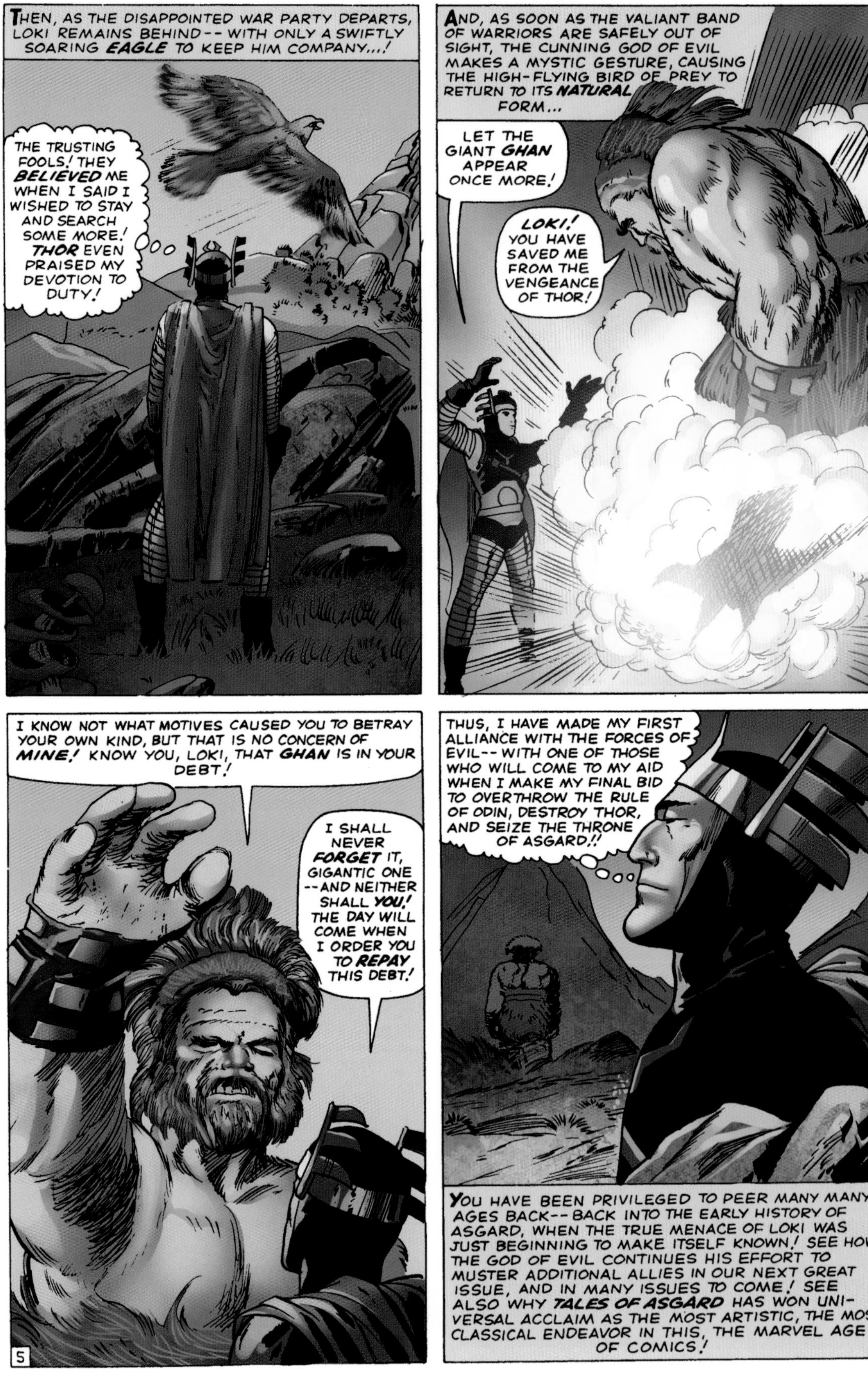
THEN, AS THE DISAPPOINTED WAR PARTY DEPARTS, LOKI REMAINS BEHIND-- WITH ONLY A SWIFTLY SOARING EAGLE TO KEEP HIM COMPANY...!
THE TRUSTING FOOLS! THEY BELIEVED ME WHEN I SAID I WISHED TO STAY AND SEARCH SOME MORE! THOR EVEN PRAISED MY DEVOTION TO DUTY!
AND, AS SOON AS THE VALIANT BAND OF WARRIORS ARE SAFELY OUT OF SIGHT, THE CUNNING GOD OF EVIL MAKES A MYSTIC GESTURE, CAUSING THE HIGH-FLYING BIRD OF PREY TO RETURN TO ITS NATURAL FORM...
LET THE GIANT GHAN APPEAR ONCE MORE!
LOKI! YOU HAVE SAVED ME FROM THE VENGEANCE OF THOR!
I KNOW NOT WHAT MOTIVES CAUSED YOU TO BETRAY YOUR OWN KIND, BUT THAT IS NO CONCERN OF MINE! KNOW YOU, LOKI, THAT GHAN IS IN YOUR DEBT!
I SHALL NEVER FORGET IT, GIGANTIC ONE --AND NEITHER SHALL YOU! THE DAY WILL COME WHEN I ORDER YOU TO REPAY THIS DEBT!
5
THUS, I HAVE MADE MY FIRST ALLIANCE WITH THE FORCES OF EVIL-- WITH ONE OF THOSE WHO WILL COME TO MY AID WHEN I MAKE MY FINAL BID TO OVERTHROW THE RULE OF ODIN, DESTROY THOR, AND SEIZE THE THRONE OF ASGARD!!
YOU HAVE BEEN PRIVILEGED TO PEER MANY MANY AGES BACK-- BACK INTO THE EARLY HISTORY OF ASGARD, WHEN THE TRUE MENACE OF LOKI WAS JUST BEGINNING TO MAKE ITSELF KNOWN! SEE HOW THE GOD OF EVIL CONTINUES HIS EFFORT TO MUSTER ADDITIONAL ALLIES IN OUR NEXT GREAT ISSUE, AND IN MANY ISSUES TO COME! SEE ALSO WHY TALES OF ASGARD HAS WON UNIVERSAL ACCLAIM AS THE MOST ARTISTIC, THE MOST CLASSICAL ENDEAVOR IN THIS, THE MARVEL AGE OF COMICS!

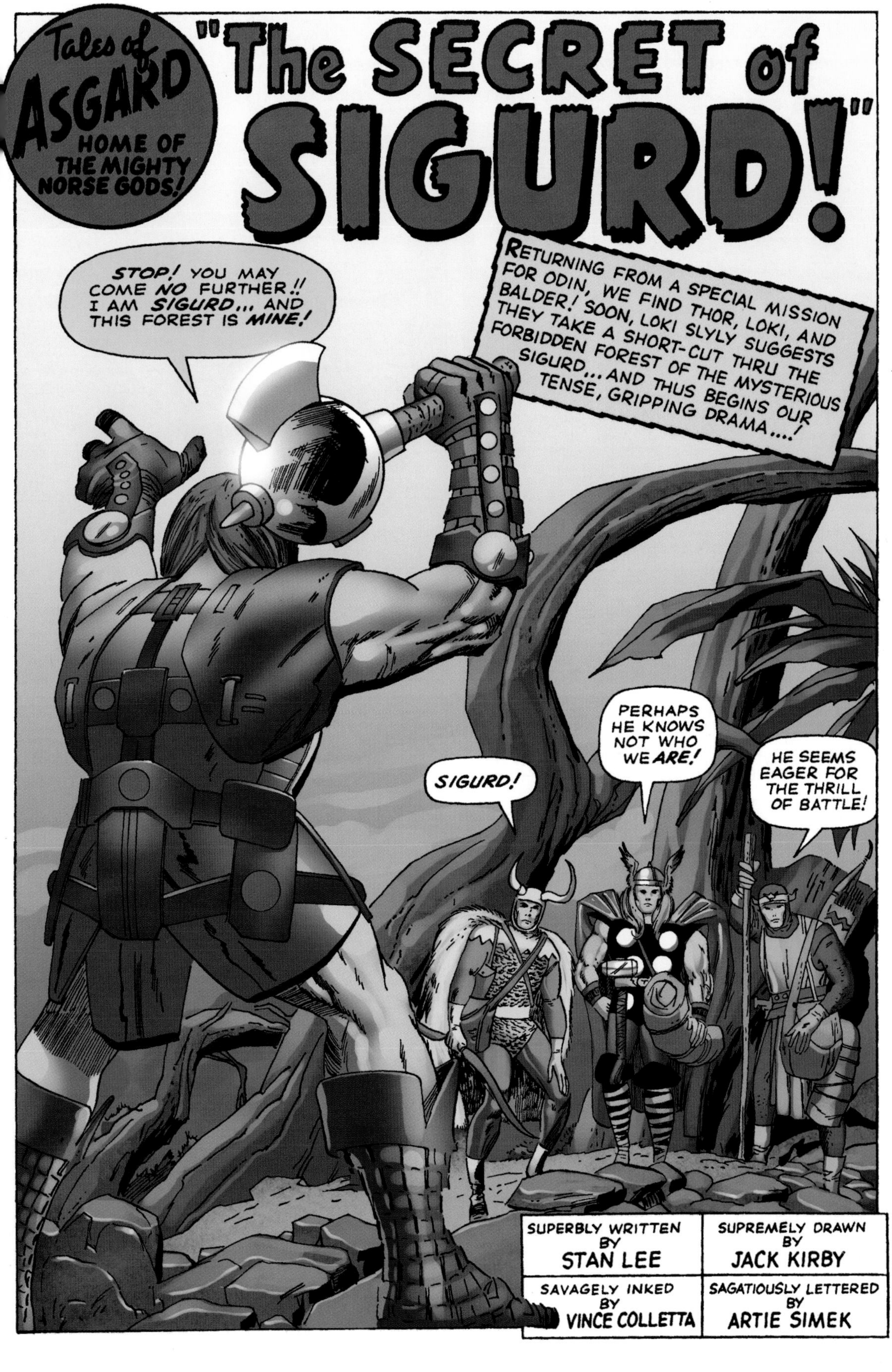

Tales of ASGARD
HOME OF THE MIGHTY NORSE GODS!
"The SECRET of SIGURD!"
STOP! YOU MAY COME NO FURTHER!! I AM SIGURD... AND THIS FOREST IS MINE!
RETURNING FROM A SPECIAL MISSION FOR ODIN, WE FIND THOR, LOKI, AND BALDER! SOON, LOKI SLYLY SUGGESTS THEY TAKE A SHORT-CUT THRU THE FORBIDDEN FOREST OF THE MYSTERIOUS SIGURD... AND THUS BEGINS OUR TENSE, GRIPPING DRAMA....!
SIGURD!
PERHAPS HE KNOWS NOT WHO WE ARE!
HE SEEMS EAGER FOR THE THRILL OF BATTLE!
SUPERBLY WRITTEN BY STAN LEE
SUPREMELY DRAWN BY JACK KIRBY
SAVAGELY INKED BY VINCE COLLETTA
SAGATIOUSLY LETTERED BY ARTIE SIMEK

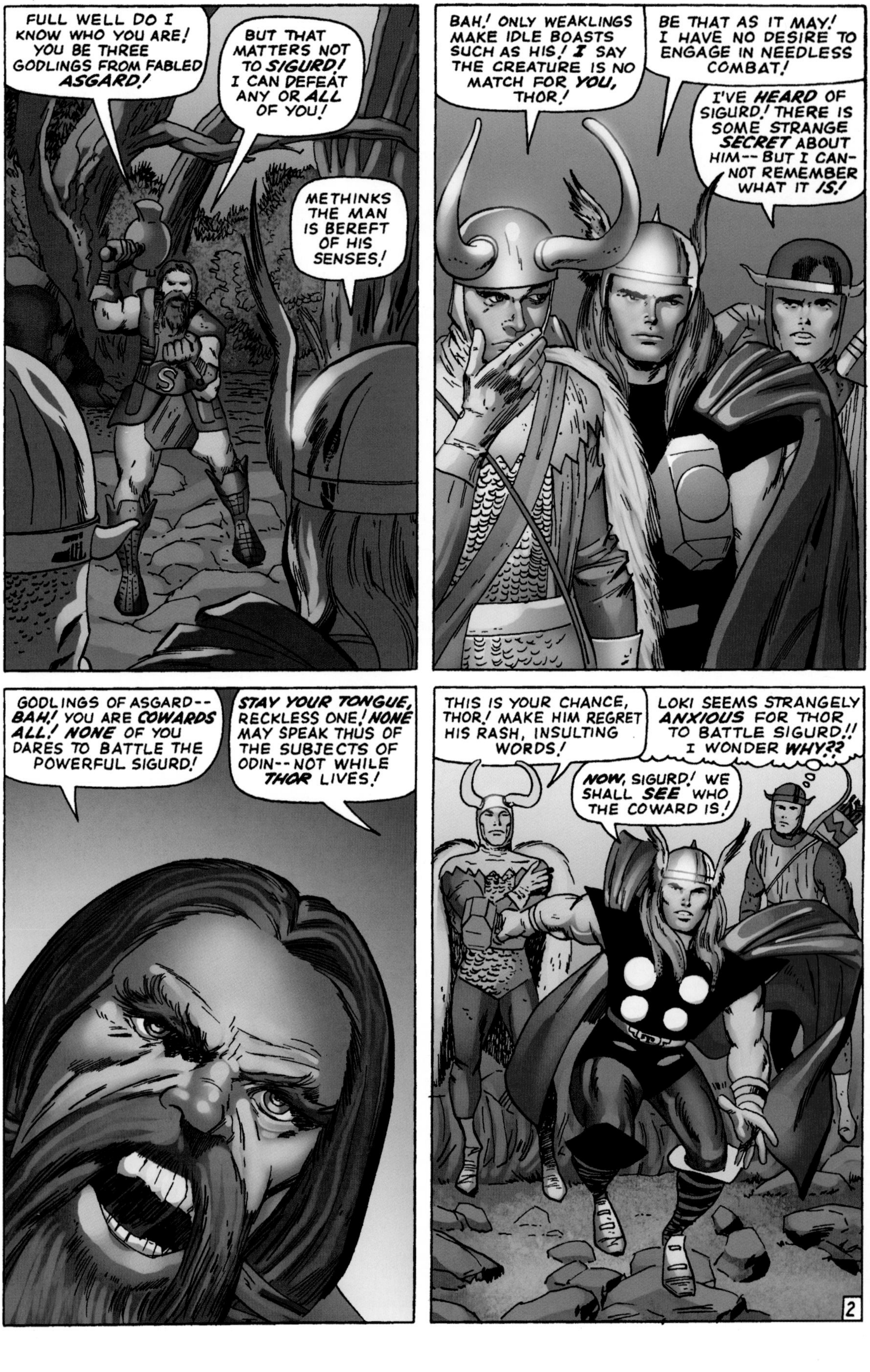

FULL WELL DO I KNOW WHO YOU ARE! YOU BE THREE GODLINGS FROM FABLED ASGARD!
BUT THAT MATTERS NOT TO SIGURD! I CAN DEFEAT ANY OR ALL OF YOU!
METHINKS THE MAN IS BEREFT OF HIS SENSES!
BAH! ONLY WEAKLINGS MAKE IDLE BOASTS SUCH AS HIS! I SAY THE CREATURE IS NO MATCH FOR YOU, THOR!
BE THAT AS IT MAY! I HAVE NO DESIRE TO ENGAGE IN NEEDLESS COMBAT!
I'VE HEARD OF SIGURD! THERE IS SOME STRANGE SECRET ABOUT HIM-- BUT I CANNOT REMEMBER WHAT IT IS!
GODLINGS OF ASGARD-- BAH! YOU ARE COWARDS ALL! NONE OF YOU DARES TO BATTLE THE POWERFUL SIGURD!
STAY YOUR TONGUE, RECKLESS ONE! NONE MAY SPEAK THUS OF THE SUBJECTS OF ODIN-- NOT WHILE THOR LIVES!
THIS IS YOUR CHANCE, THOR! MAKE HIM REGRET HIS RASH, INSULTING WORDS!
LOKI SEEMS STRANGELY ANXIOUS FOR THOR TO BATTLE SIGURD!! I WONDER WHY??
NOW, SIGURD! WE SHALL SEE WHO THE COWARD IS!
2

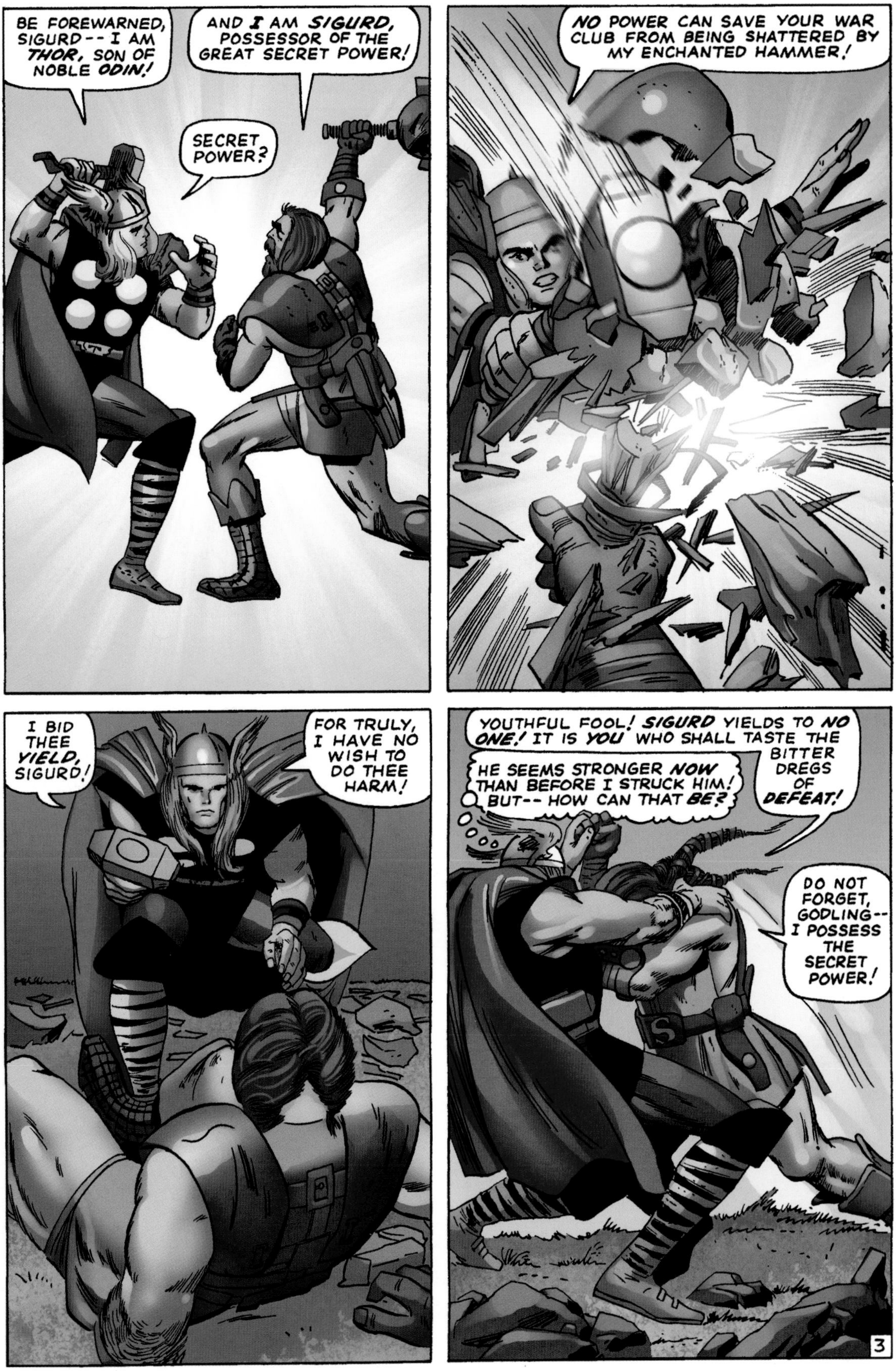
BE FOREWARNED, SIGURD -- I AM THOR, SON OF NOBLE ODIN!
AND I AM SIGURD, POSSESSOR OF THE GREAT SECRET POWER!
SECRET POWER?
NO POWER CAN SAVE YOUR WAR CLUB FROM BEING SHATTERED BY MY ENCHANTED HAMMER!
I BID THEE YIELD, SIGURD!
FOR TRULY, I HAVE NO WISH TO DO THEE HARM!
YOUTHFUL FOOL! SIGURD YIELDS TO NO ONE! IT IS YOU WHO SHALL TASTE THE BITTER DREGS OF DEFEAT!
HE SEEMS STRONGER NOW THAN BEFORE I STRUCK HIM! BUT-- HOW CAN THAT BE?
DO NOT FORGET, GODLING-- I POSSESS THE SECRET POWER!
3

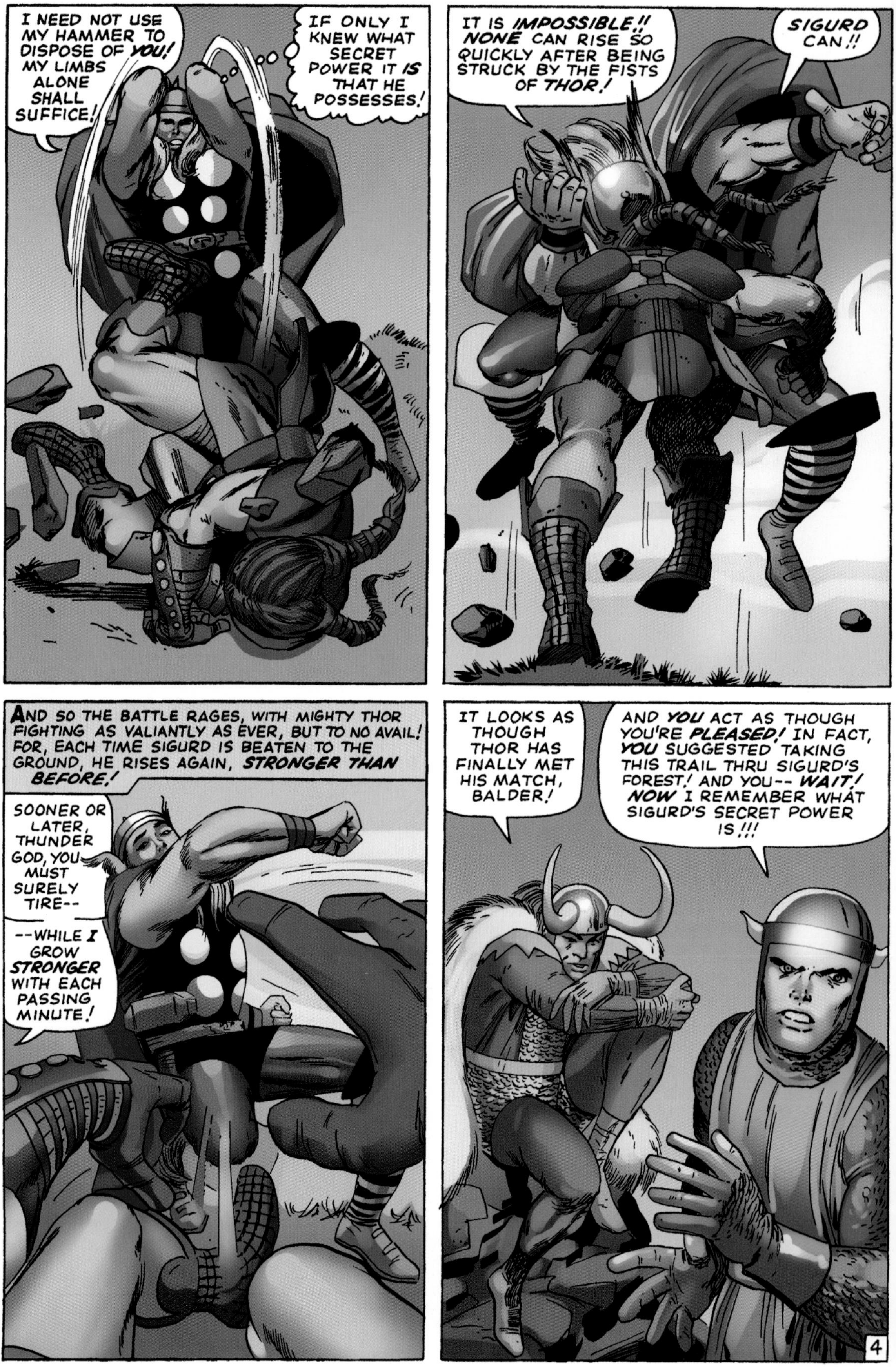

I NEED NOT USE MY HAMMER TO DISPOSE OF YOU! MY LIMBS ALONE SHALL SUFFICE!
IF ONLY I KNEW WHAT SECRET POWER IT IS THAT HE POSSESSES!
IT IS IMPOSSIBLE!! NONE CAN RISE SO QUICKLY AFTER BEING STRUCK BY THE FISTS OF THOR!
SIGURD CAN!!
AND SO THE BATTLE RAGES, WITH MIGHTY THOR FIGHTING AS VALIANTLY AS EVER, BUT TO NO AVAIL! FOR, EACH TIME SIGURD IS BEATEN TO THE GROUND, HE RISES AGAIN, STRONGER THAN BEFORE!
SOONER OR LATER, THUNDER GOD, YOU MUST SURELY TIRE--
--WHILE I GROW STRONGER WITH EACH PASSING MINUTE!
IT LOOKS AS THOUGH THOR HAS FINALLY MET HIS MATCH, BALDER!
AND YOU ACT AS THOUGH YOU'RE PLEASED! IN FACT, YOU SUGGESTED TAKING THIS TRAIL THRU SIGURD'S FOREST! AND YOU-- WAIT! NOW I REMEMBER WHAT SIGURD'S SECRET POWER IS!!!
4

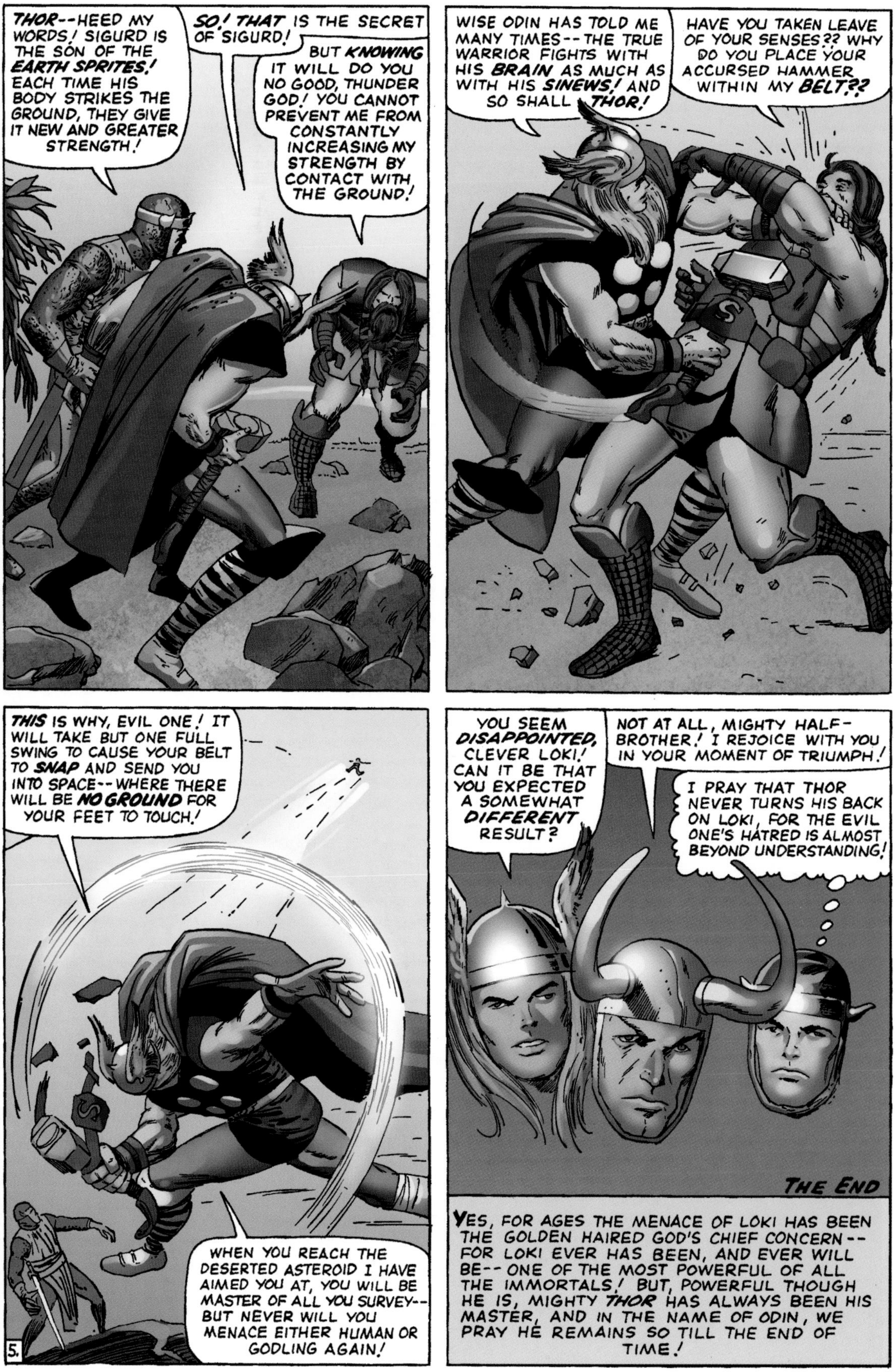
THOR--HEED MY WORDS! SIGURD IS THE SON OF THE EARTH SPRITES! EACH TIME HIS BODY STRIKES THE GROUND, THEY GIVE IT NEW AND GREATER STRENGTH!
SO! THAT IS THE SECRET OF SIGURD!
BUT KNOWING IT WILL DO YOU NO GOOD, THUNDER GOD! YOU CANNOT PREVENT ME FROM CONSTANTLY INCREASING MY STRENGTH BY CONTACT WITH THE GROUND!
WISE ODIN HAS TOLD ME MANY TIMES--THE TRUE WARRIOR FIGHTS WITH HIS BRAIN AS MUCH AS WITH HIS SINEWS! AND SO SHALL THOR!
HAVE YOU TAKEN LEAVE OF YOUR SENSES?? WHY DO YOU PLACE YOUR ACCURSED HAMMER WITHIN MY BELT??
THIS IS WHY, EVIL ONE! IT WILL TAKE BUT ONE FULL SWING TO CAUSE YOUR BELT TO SNAP AND SEND YOU INTO SPACE--WHERE THERE WILL BE NO GROUND FOR YOUR FEET TO TOUCH!
WHEN YOU REACH THE DESERTED ASTEROID I HAVE AIMED YOU AT, YOU WILL BE MASTER OF ALL YOU SURVEY--BUT NEVER WILL YOU MENACE EITHER HUMAN OR GODLING AGAIN!
5.
YOU SEEM DISAPPOINTED, CLEVER LOKI! CAN IT BE THAT YOU EXPECTED A SOMEWHAT DIFFERENT RESULT?
NOT AT ALL, MIGHTY HALF-BROTHER! I REJOICE WITH YOU IN YOUR MOMENT OF TRIUMPH!
I PRAY THAT THOR NEVER TURNS HIS BACK ON LOKI, FOR THE EVIL ONE'S HATRED IS ALMOST BEYOND UNDERSTANDING!
THE END
YES, FOR AGES THE MENACE OF LOKI HAS BEEN THE GOLDEN HAIRED GOD'S CHIEF CONCERN--FOR LOKI EVER HAS BEEN, AND EVER WILL BE--ONE OF THE MOST POWERFUL OF ALL THE IMMORTALS! BUT, POWERFUL THOUGH HE IS, MIGHTY THOR HAS ALWAYS BEEN HIS MASTER, AND IN THE NAME OF ODIN, WE PRAY HE REMAINS SO TILL THE END OF TIME!

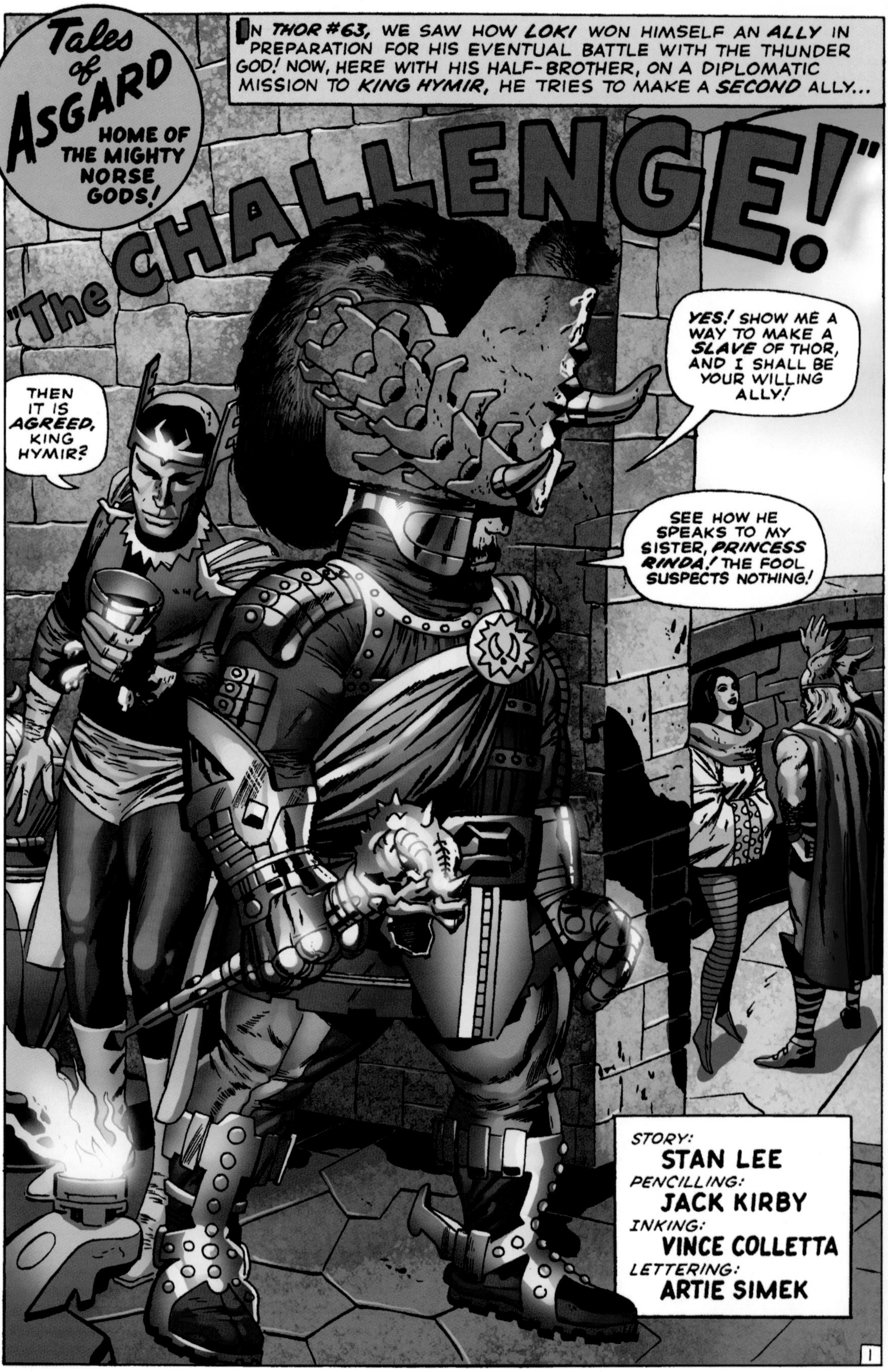
Tales of ASGARD HOME OF THE MIGHTY NORSE GODS!
IN THOR #63, WE SAW HOW LOKI WON HIMSELF AN ALLY IN PREPARATION FOR HIS EVENTUAL BATTLE WITH THE THUNDER GOD! NOW, HERE WITH HIS HALF-BROTHER, ON A DIPLOMATIC MISSION TO KING HYMIR, HE TRIES TO MAKE A SECOND ALLY...
"The CHALLENGE!"
THEN IT IS AGREED, KING HYMIR?
YES! SHOW ME A WAY TO MAKE A SLAVE OF THOR, AND I SHALL BE YOUR WILLING ALLY!
SEE HOW HE SPEAKS TO MY SISTER, PRINCESS RINDA! THE FOOL SUSPECTS NOTHING!
STORY: STAN LEE
PENCILLING: JACK KIRBY
INKING: VINCE COLLETTA
LETTERING: ARTIE SIMEK
1

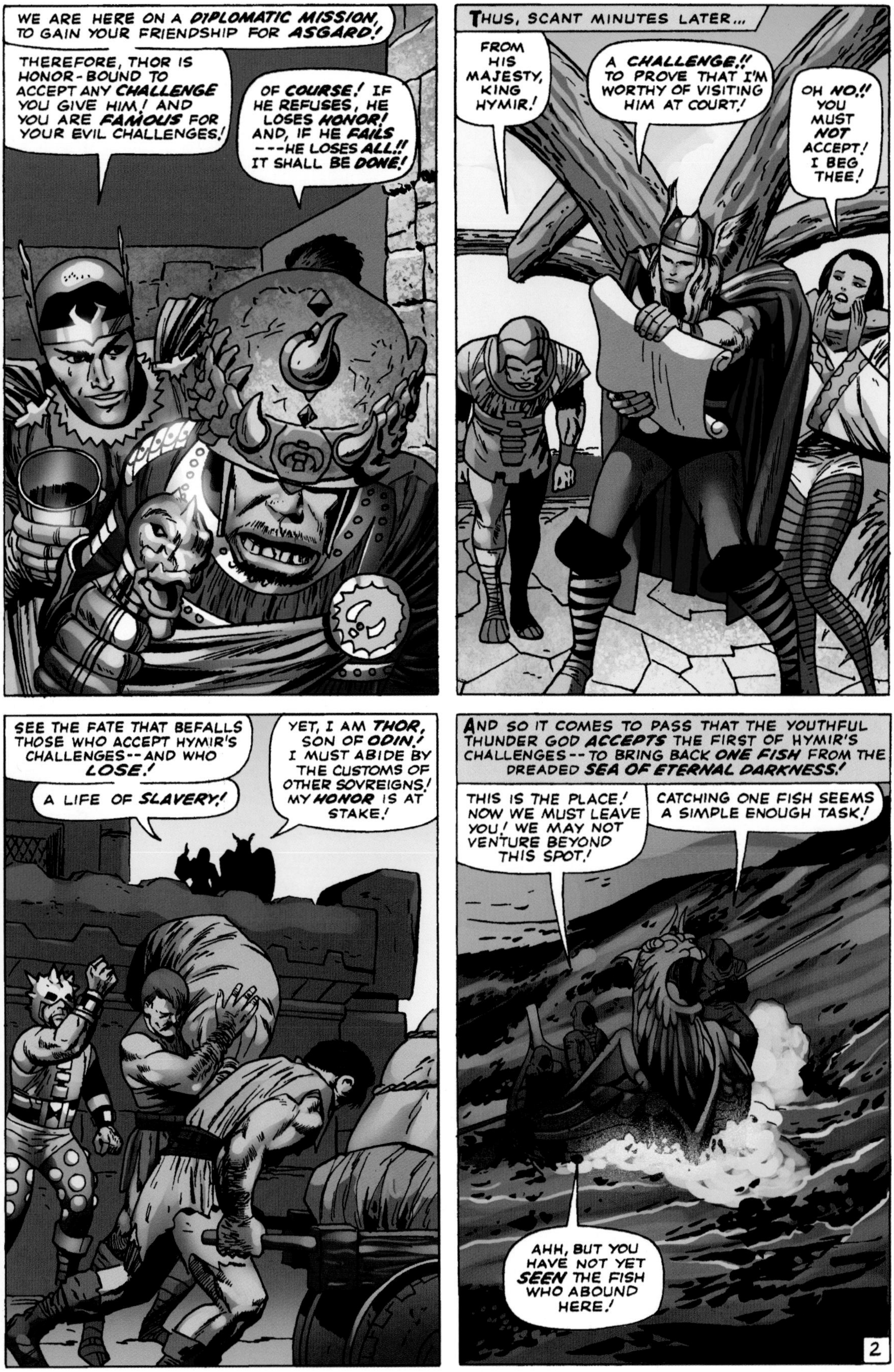
WE ARE HERE ON A DIPLOMATIC MISSION, TO GAIN YOUR FRIENDSHIP FOR ASGARD!
THEREFORE, THOR IS HONOR-BOUND TO ACCEPT ANY CHALLENGE YOU GIVE HIM! AND YOU ARE FAMOUS FOR YOUR EVIL CHALLENGES!
OF COURSE! IF HE REFUSES, HE LOSES HONOR! AND, IF HE FAILS---HE LOSES ALL!! IT SHALL BE DONE!
THUS, SCANT MINUTES LATER...
FROM HIS MAJESTY, KING HYMIR!
A CHALLENGE!! TO PROVE THAT I'M WORTHY OF VISITING HIM AT COURT!
OH NO!! YOU MUST NOT ACCEPT! I BEG THEE!
SEE THE FATE THAT BEFALLS THOSE WHO ACCEPT HYMIR'S CHALLENGES--AND WHO LOSE!
A LIFE OF SLAVERY!
YET, I AM THOR, SON OF ODIN! I MUST ABIDE BY THE CUSTOMS OF OTHER SOVREIGNS! MY HONOR IS AT STAKE!
AND SO IT COMES TO PASS THAT THE YOUTHFUL THUNDER GOD ACCEPTS THE FIRST OF HYMIR'S CHALLENGES--TO BRING BACK ONE FISH FROM THE DREADED SEA OF ETERNAL DARKNESS!
THIS IS THE PLACE! NOW WE MUST LEAVE YOU! WE MAY NOT VENTURE BEYOND THIS SPOT!
CATCHING ONE FISH SEEMS A SIMPLE ENOUGH TASK!
AHH, BUT YOU HAVE NOT YET SEEN THE FISH WHO ABOUND HERE!
2

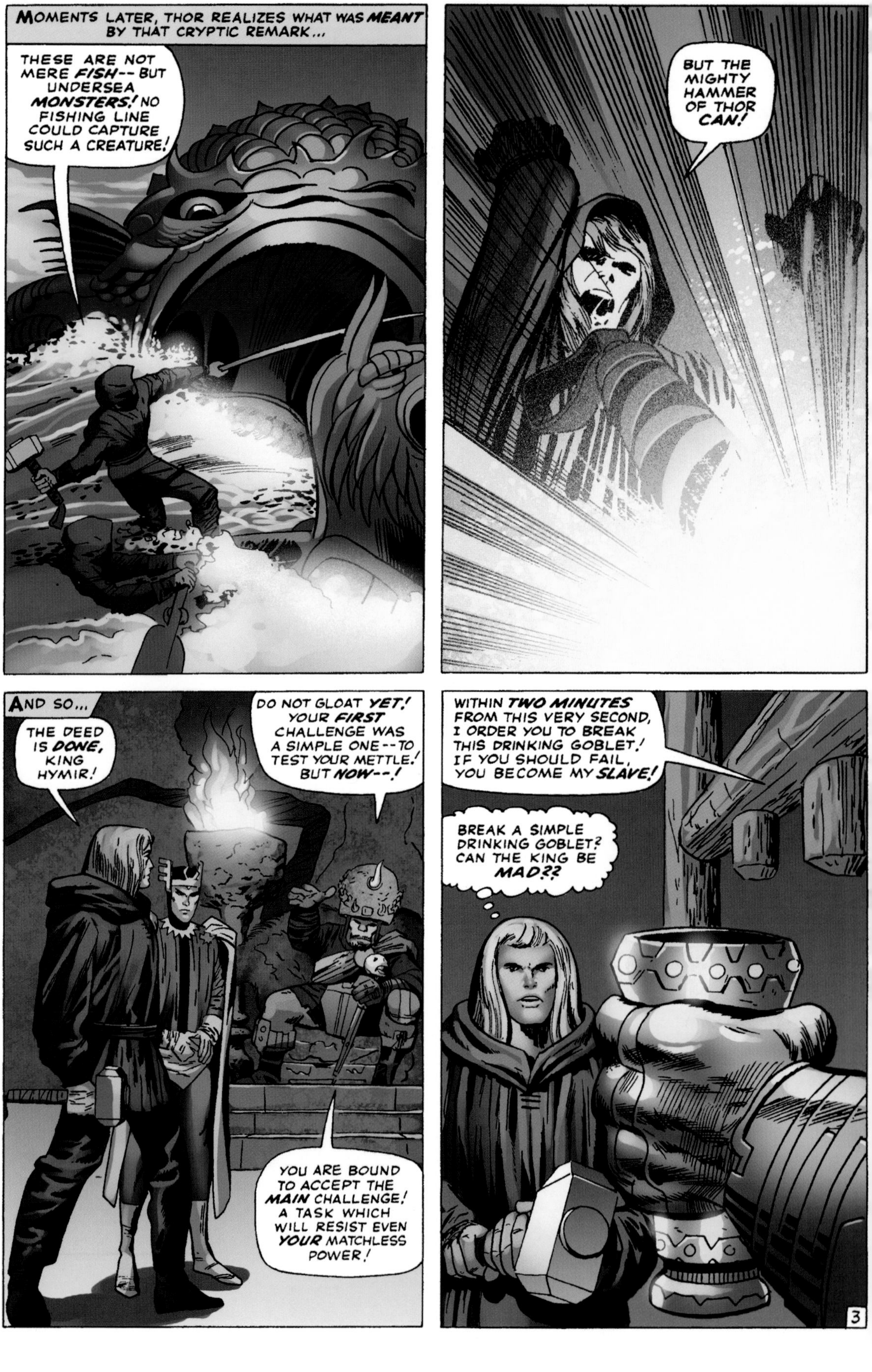
MOMENTS LATER, THOR REALIZES WHAT WAS MEANT BY THAT CRYPTIC REMARK...
THESE ARE NOT MERE FISH-- BUT UNDERSEA MONSTERS! NO FISHING LINE COULD CAPTURE SUCH A CREATURE!
BUT THE MIGHTY HAMMER OF THOR CAN!
AND SO...
THE DEED IS DONE, KING HYMIR!
DO NOT GLOAT YET! YOUR FIRST CHALLENGE WAS A SIMPLE ONE -- TO TEST YOUR METTLE! BUT NOW--!
YOU ARE BOUND TO ACCEPT THE MAIN CHALLENGE! A TASK WHICH WILL RESIST EVEN YOUR MATCHLESS POWER!
WITHIN TWO MINUTES FROM THIS VERY SECOND, I ORDER YOU TO BREAK THIS DRINKING GOBLET! IF YOU SHOULD FAIL, YOU BECOME MY SLAVE!
BREAK A SIMPLE DRINKING GOBLET? CAN THE KING BE MAD??
3

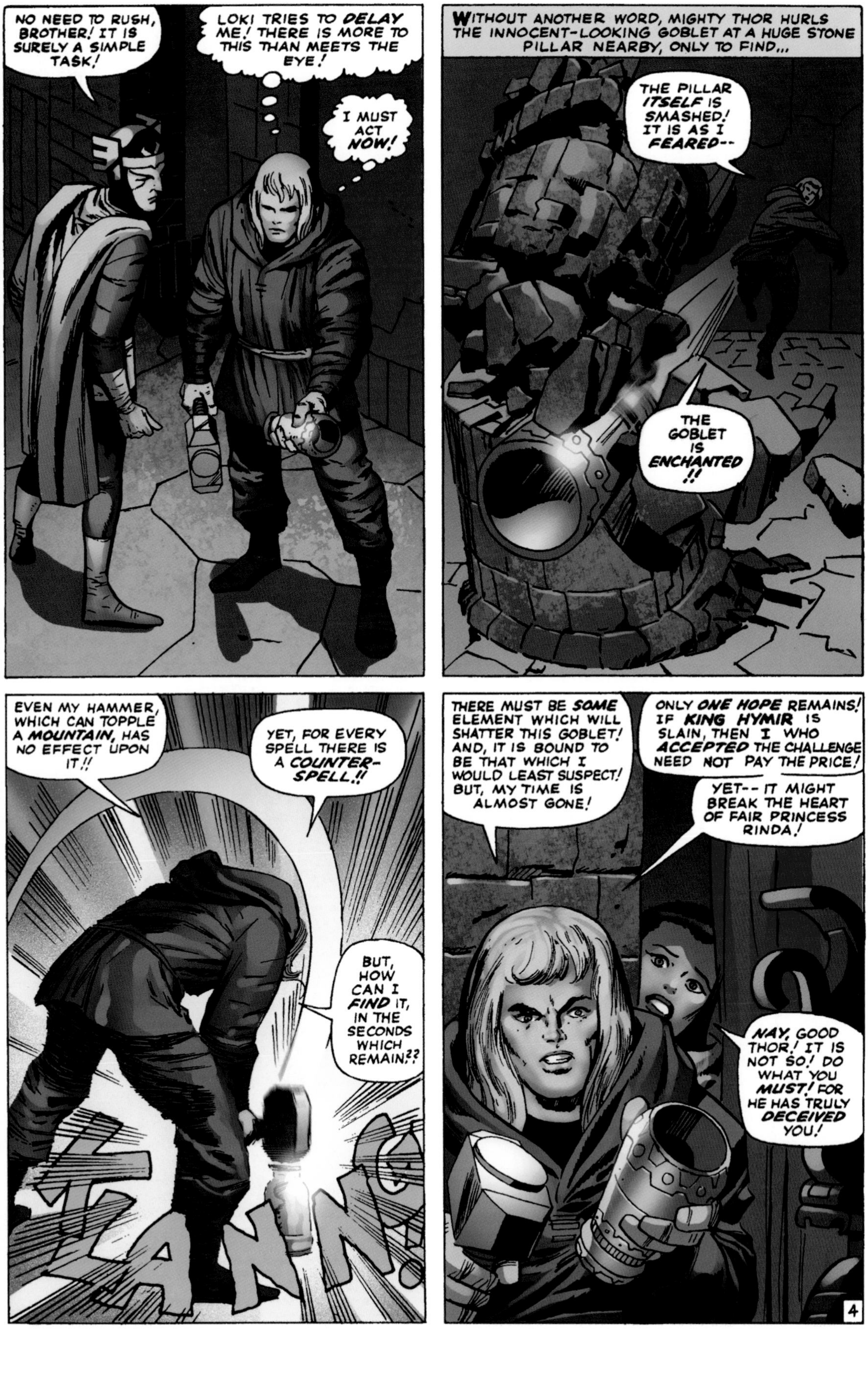

NO NEED TO RUSH, BROTHER! IT IS SURELY A SIMPLE TASK!
LOKI TRIES TO *DELAY* ME! THERE IS MORE TO THIS THAN MEETS THE EYE!
I MUST ACT *NOW!*
WITHOUT ANOTHER WORD, MIGHTY THOR HURLS THE INNOCENT-LOOKING GOBLET AT A HUGE STONE PILLAR NEARBY, ONLY TO FIND...
THE PILLAR *ITSELF* IS SMASHED! IT IS AS I *FEARED--*
THE GOBLET IS *ENCHANTED!!*
EVEN MY HAMMER, WHICH CAN TOPPLE A *MOUNTAIN*, HAS NO EFFECT UPON IT!!
YET, FOR EVERY SPELL THERE IS A *COUNTER-SPELL!!*
BUT, HOW CAN I *FIND* IT, IN THE SECONDS WHICH REMAIN??
THERE MUST BE *SOME* ELEMENT WHICH WILL SHATTER THIS GOBLET! AND, IT IS BOUND TO BE THAT WHICH I WOULD LEAST SUSPECT! BUT, MY TIME IS ALMOST GONE!
ONLY *ONE HOPE* REMAINS! IF *KING HYMIR* IS SLAIN, THEN *I* WHO *ACCEPTED* THE CHALLENGE NEED NOT PAY THE PRICE!
YET-- IT MIGHT BREAK THE HEART OF FAIR PRINCESS RINDA!
NAY, GOOD THOR! IT IS NOT SO! DO WHAT YOU *MUST!* FOR HE HAS TRULY *DECEIVED* YOU!
4

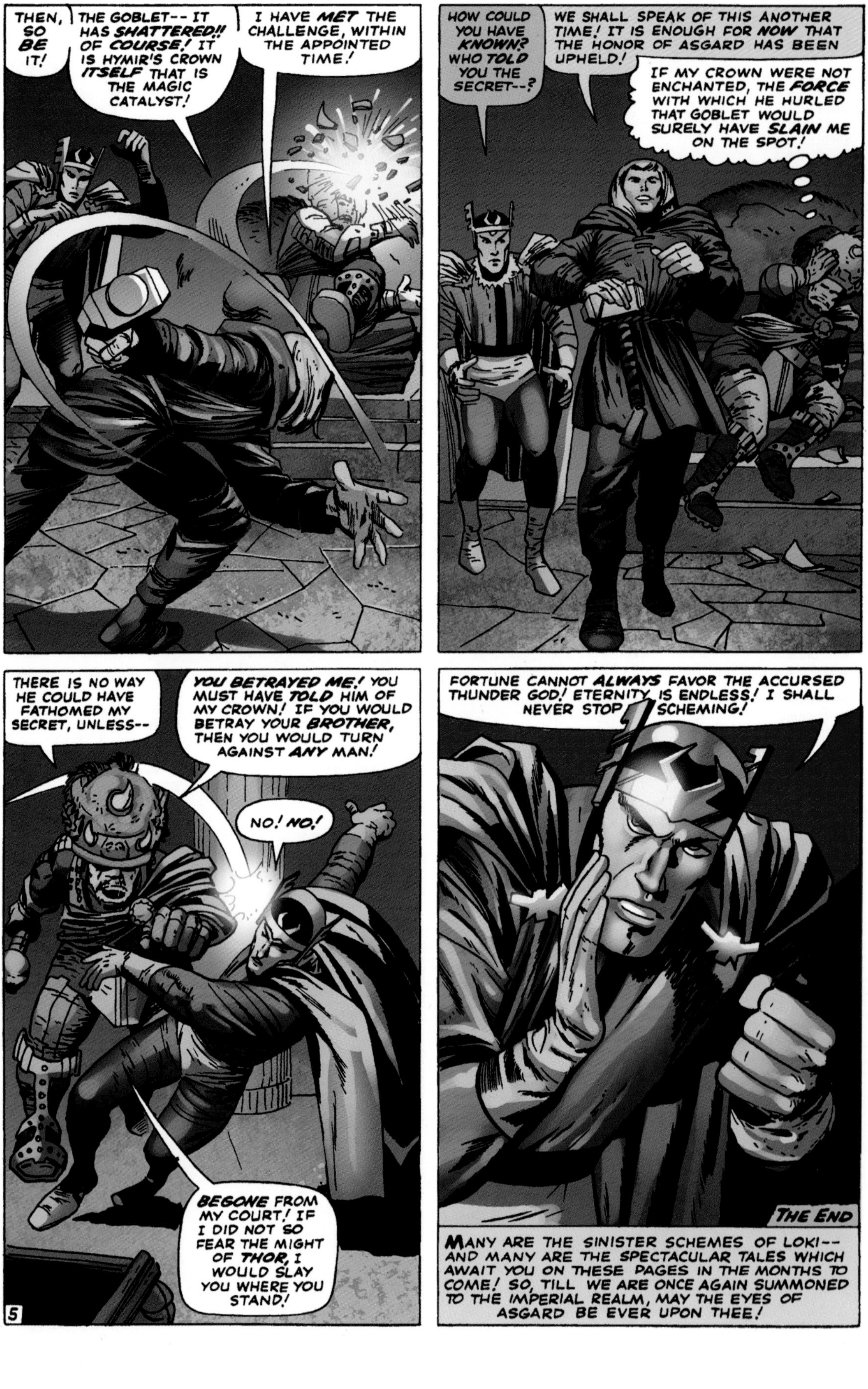
THEN, SO BE IT!
THE GOBLET-- IT HAS SHATTERED!! OF COURSE! IT IS HYMIR'S CROWN ITSELF THAT IS THE MAGIC CATALYST!
I HAVE MET THE CHALLENGE, WITHIN THE APPOINTED TIME!
HOW COULD YOU HAVE KNOWN? WHO TOLD YOU THE SECRET--?
WE SHALL SPEAK OF THIS ANOTHER TIME! IT IS ENOUGH FOR NOW THAT THE HONOR OF ASGARD HAS BEEN UPHELD!
IF MY CROWN WERE NOT ENCHANTED, THE FORCE WITH WHICH HE HURLED THAT GOBLET WOULD SURELY HAVE SLAIN ME ON THE SPOT!
THERE IS NO WAY HE COULD HAVE FATHOMED MY SECRET, UNLESS--
YOU BETRAYED ME! YOU MUST HAVE TOLD HIM OF MY CROWN! IF YOU WOULD BETRAY YOUR BROTHER, THEN YOU WOULD TURN AGAINST ANY MAN!
NO! NO!
BEGONE FROM MY COURT! IF I DID NOT SO FEAR THE MIGHT OF THOR, I WOULD SLAY YOU WHERE YOU STAND!
5
FORTUNE CANNOT ALWAYS FAVOR THE ACCURSED THUNDER GOD! ETERNITY IS ENDLESS! I SHALL NEVER STOP SCHEMING!
THE END
MANY ARE THE SINISTER SCHEMES OF LOKI-- AND MANY ARE THE SPECTACULAR TALES WHICH AWAIT YOU ON THESE PAGES IN THE MONTHS TO COME! SO, TILL WE ARE ONCE AGAIN SUMMONED TO THE IMPERIAL REALM, MAY THE EYES OF ASGARD BE EVER UPON THEE!

LOKI

Real Name: Loki Laufeyson
Occupation: God of Mischief
Identity: Publicly known to citizens of Asgard. His existence is not known to the general public of Earth.
Legal status: Citizen of Asgard (often in exile)
Former aliases: As a shape-changer, Loki has impersonated a vast number of individuals and things.
Place of birth: Jotunheim
Marital status: Separated
Known relatives: Sigyn (wife, separated), Laufey (father, deceased), Farbauti (mother), Odin (foster father), Frigga (foster mother), Thor (foster brother)
Group affiliation: Sometime ally of Karnilla, the Enchantress, the Executioner, the Absorbing Man, and Lorelei, former ally of Dormammu
Base of operations: A castle on the outskirts of Asgard
First appearance: JOURNEY INTO MYSTERY #85
Origin: JOURNEY INTO MYSTERY #112, 113, 115
History: Loki is the son of Laufey, king of the frost giants of Jotunheim, one of the "Nine Worlds" of the Asgardian cosmology (see *Asgard, Asgardians*). Odin, ruler of Asgard, led his subjects in a war against the giants (see *Odin*). Laufey was slain in battle and the giants were defeated. Surveying the spoils of war, the Asgardians discovered a small god-sized baby hidden at the giants' main fortress. The infant was Loki, whom Laufey had kept hidden due to his shame over his son's diminutive size. Because Loki was the son of a king fallen in battle, Odin elected to adopt him and raise him as a son alongside his bloodson Thor, the future god of thunder (see *Thor*).

In childhood Loki greatly resented the fact that Odin and the other Asgardians favored the young Thor, who already had a nobility of spirit and excelled in all his endeavors, over himself. As a boy Loki began studying the arts of sorcery, for which he had a natural affinity. His hatred of Thor grew, and while still a boy, Loki vowed to become the most powerful god in Asgard and to destroy Thor in order to achieve this end. Ater achieving adulthood Loki began making alliances with other enemies of Asgard.

As Loki grew to adulthood, his inborn propensity for mischief had begun to manifest itself, and he earned the nickname "God of Mischief." But as his deeds grew increasingly malicious, and his lust for power and vengeance became apparent, he became known as the "God of Evil". Loki attempted many times over the centuries to destroy Thor and seize the throne of Asgard for himself. Finally, Odin magically imprisoned him within a tree as punishment for his many crimes. Sometime thereafter, Thor was banished to Earth to learn humility in the mortal form of Dr. Donald Blake.

Shortly after Blake regained the ability to assume the godly form and power of Thor, Loki succeeded in freeding himself from his mystical imprisonment. There followed a long succession of clashes between Loki and Thor. Sometimes Loki battled Thor directly. On other occasions Loki used pawns to fight Thor, some of whom he temporarily endowed with increased superhuman power, such as the Cobra and Mister Hyde (see individual entries). Loki is responsible for transforming "Crusher" Creel into the Absorbing Man and for the revival of the

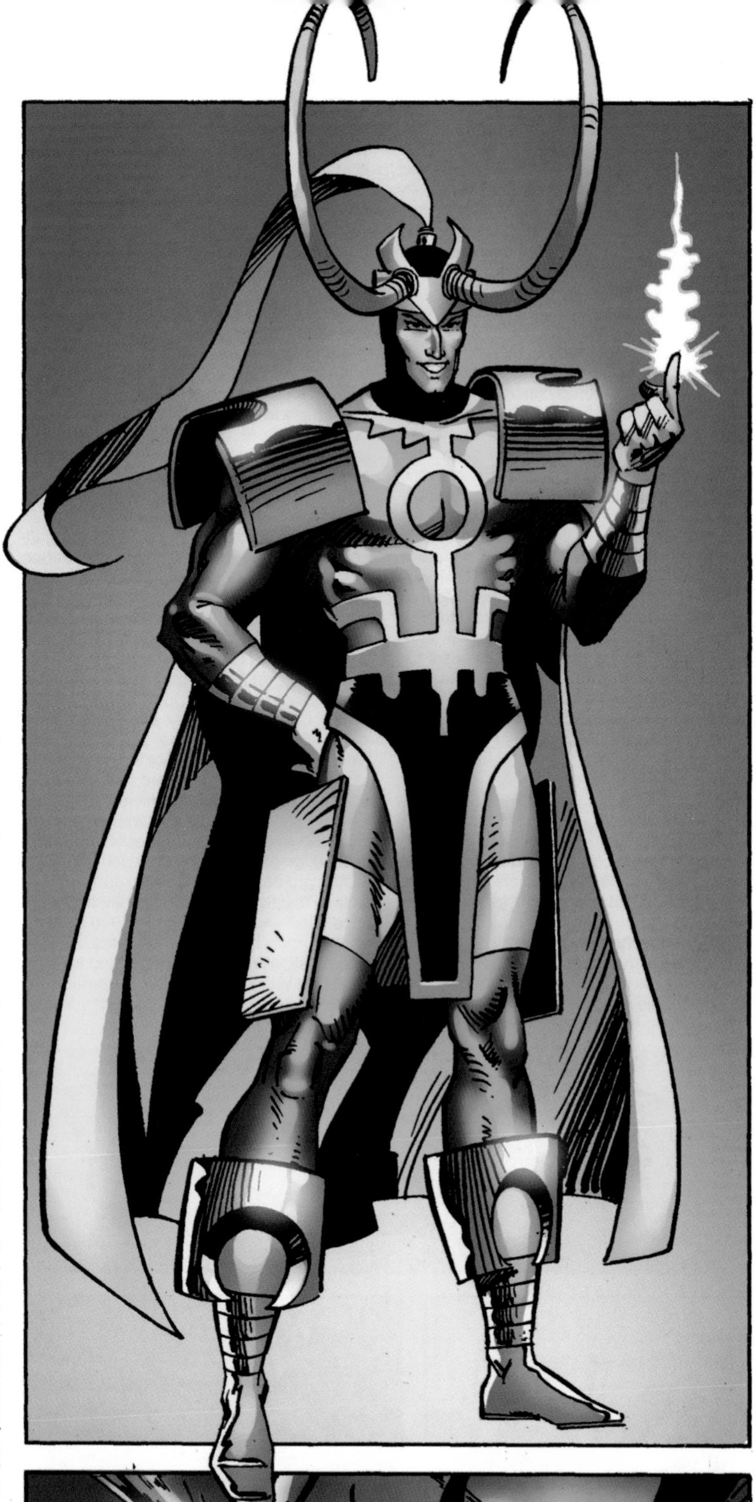

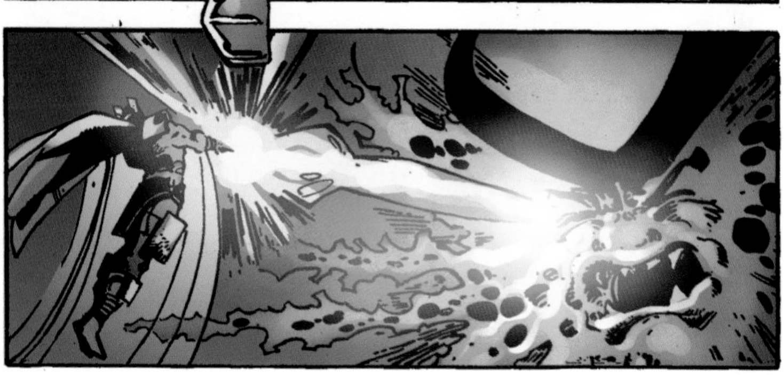

Asgardian Destroyer as an opponent for Thor (see *Absorbing Man, Destroyed: Destroyer*). Loki has attempted to turn Odin against Thor and to steal Thor's enchanted hammer. On one occasion Loki mystically exchanged bodies with Thor. Loki has temporarily seized control of Asgard when Odin was incapacitated. However, Loki has invariably been thwarted in his bids for power and revenge by Thor.

Recently, Loki joined Thor and Odin in their battle against the demonic Surtur (see *Surtur*). Surtur intended to destroy Asgard, and Loki, whose goal is to rule Asgard, therefore felt obliged to stop him. After Odin and Surtur vanished at the end of this battle, Loki began his machinations to be named as the new ruler of Asgard. As part of his plans he magically transformed Thor into a frog, using power drawn from Surtur's abandoned sword. But Thor was returned to his normal form when the Asgardian Volstagg destroyed the engine draining power from the sword (see *Warriors Three*). Loki was unable to prevent the ascension of Balder to the Asgardian throne after Thor refused the throne himself (see *Balder*).

However, Loki is continuing his quest for supreme power in Asgard. It has been said that should the time of Ragnarok, the destruction of the Asgardian gods ever come, Loki will lead the forces of evil against Asgard.

Height: 6′ 4″
Weight: 525 lbs
Eyes: Green
Hair: Black-grey
Strength level: Loki possesses the normal strength of an Asgardian male of his age, height, and build. He can lift (press) about 30 tons.

Known superhuman powers: Loki possesses the conventional attributes of an Asgardian, as well as certain innate magical powers. Like all Asgardians, Loki is extremely long-lived (though not immortal like

the Olympians), superhumanly strong, immune to all diseases, and resistant to conventional injury. (Asgardian flesh and bone is about 3 times denser than similar human tissue, contributing to the Asgardian's superhuman strength and weight.) His Asgardian metabolism gives him superhuman endurance in all physical activities.

Besides these physical abilities, Loki possesses a host of magical skills. Among these is his ability to transform his shape at will into those of other creatures. He has become such animals as a snake, eagle, mouse, and bee, gaining the basic natural abilities inherent in each form. While he can take on the likeness of another god, giant, or human, he will not necessarily gain the special physical or mental powers of the being he imitates. Loki can also transform external objects into other forms and substances by magic; for instance, he can turn clouds into dragons. He can also bring inanimate objects to life, or mystically imbue objects or beings with specific but temporary powers. He has, for example, augmented the might of such human criminals as the Cobra and Sandu (see *Cobra, Appendix: Sandu*). These magical effects remain only for as long as he maintains the spell that created them.

Loki can project highly powerful concussive bolts of mystical energy. He can also create magical energy fields which serve various purposes. With great concentration, Loki can create a field of sufficient resilience to repel Thor's enchanted hammer (though repeated blows would undoubtedly penetrate it) or physical objects such as large-caliber projectiles. He can also surround objects in mystical energy to levitate them. He once lifted and supported an entire building off the ground for several minutes. He can also mystically levitate himself and thereby fly at great speed. As with his influence over matter, his magical energy feats only last as long as he maintains them.

Loki also has a number of mental and extrasensory powers which are analogous to psionic abilities. He can broadcast his thoughts into other minds as well as plant compelling hypnotic suggestions. These telepathic abilities do not appear to be limited by distance: Loki can even cast his thoughts across dimensions. Loki cannot, however, perceive the thoughts of others. He does have certain extrasensory powers of perception, however, enabling him to see and hear events in distant places simultaneous to their occurrence. He can also mentally project an image of himself, in a manner not unlike astral projection, through which he can communicate with beings in other places.

Loki can also magically create rifts between dimensions, allowing him or other objects passage from one universe to another. Most often this rift is between Asgard and Earth.

Loki also has a vast knowledge of spells which he can use for many magical effects.

Loki has used his magic to enable him to endure injuries with little or no effect which would kill another Asgardian. He has even been beheaded, and yet he continued to live, magically reattached his head to his body, and was in the same condition as he was in before the beheading.

Weapons: Loki occasionally employs certain magical power objects, such as the Norn Stones or rare Asgardian herbs, to augment his own magical powers. These objects or substances are generally used to enhance his immediate personal strength or abilities, or to create a permanent magical transformation, such as that which gave the Absorbing Man his power. He once used the mystical sword of Surtur along with various equipment to transform Thor into a frog while Loki was in Asgard and Thor on Earth (see *Surtur*). The destruction of the engine drawing power from the sword caused Thor to return to his normal form. ∎